"We Do Not Know Where Ghasib's Spies Are Or How Much He Knows.

"It would not be good enough for you merely to say you are with me. You would have to be actually with me here," Ashraf insisted.

"You mean, to convince them that I'm in position and can be activated whenever they choose," Dana said flatly.

Ashraf bent his head.

Dana was furious suddenly. "And what do I say when they give me a vial of poison to feed you, or ask me to take you to such and such a place so they can use you for target practice? What if they trick me? What if they've already tricked me? What if there's a bomb in my suitcase or a…an inhalant poison in my perfume or something?"

He looked at her. *Not poison, but intoxication,* he thought. *And just as dangerous.*

Dear Reader,

Welcome to Silhouette Desire, where you can indulge yourself every month with six passionate, powerful and provocative romances! And you can take romance one step further.... Look inside for details about our exciting new contest, "Silhouette Makes You a Star."

Popular author Mary Lynn Baxter returns to Desire with our MAN OF THE MONTH when *The Millionaire Comes Home* to Texas to reunite with the woman he could never forget. Rising star Sheri WhiteFeather's latest story features a *Comanche Vow* that leads to a marriage of convenience...until passionate love transforms it into the real thing.

It's our pleasure to present you with a new miniseries entitled 20 AMBER COURT, featuring four twentysomething female friends who share an address...and their discoveries about life and love. Don't miss the launch title, *When Jayne Met Erik,* by beloved author Elizabeth Bevarly. The scandalous Desire miniseries FORTUNES OF TEXAS: THE LOST HEIRS continues with *Fortune's Secret Daughter* by Barbara McCauley. Alexandra Sellers offers you another sumptuous story in her miniseries SONS OF THE DESERT: THE SULTANS, *Sleeping with the Sultan.* And the talented Cindy Gerard brings you a touching love story about a man of honor pledged to marry an innocent young woman with a secret, in *The Bridal Arrangement.*

Treat yourself to all six of these tantalizing tales from Silhouette Desire.

Enjoy!

Joan Marlow Golan

Joan Marlow Golan
Senior Editor, Silhouette Desire

Sleeping with the Sultan

ALEXANDRA SELLERS

Published by Silhouette Books

America's Publisher of Contemporary Romance

For
Leslie Wainger and Isabel Swift,
who thought I should write about sheikhs.

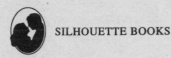 SILHOUETTE BOOKS

ISBN 0-373-76391-3

SLEEPING WITH THE SULTAN

This edition published by arrangement with Harlequin Books S.A.

® and TM are trademarks of Harlequin Books S.A., used under license. Trademarks indicated with ® are registered in the United States Patent and Trademark Office, the Canadian Trade Marks Office and in other countries.

Visit Silhouette at www.eHarlequin.com

Printed in U.S.A.

ALEXANDRA SELLERS

is the author of over twenty-five novels and a feline language text published in 1997 and still selling.

Born and raised in Canada, Alexandra first came to London as a drama student. Now she lives near Hampstead Heath with her husband, Nick. They share housekeeping with Monsieur, who jumped through the window one day and announced, as cats do, that he was moving in.

What she would miss most on a desert island is shared laughter.

Readers can write to Alexandra at P.O. Box 9449, London NW3 2WH, England.

SILHOUETTE MAKES YOU A STAR!
Feel like a star with Silhouette.
Look for the exciting details of our new contest
inside all of these fabulous Silhouette novels:

One

"Look, it's Reena!"

"She looks so different in real life!"

"What a dress!"

"Wow, she's practically *naked!*"

Dana Morningstar paused at the top of the short flight of steps leading down into the bar as the whispers ran in a little ripple around the rapidly filling room.

"Isn't she wearing *anything* under it?"

"She's *so* beautiful!"

"My dear, you are a ravishingly wanton nun tonight," said a gravelly, perfectly produced voice at her elbow, and she turned with a smile to greet one of the great theatrical "Sirs" of the old school who had entered just behind her.

"Hello, Sir Henry, how nice to see you."

"And how lovely to see you, Dana. Who, if I may ask, designed that very dashing frock for you?"

The very dashing frock consisted of a double layer of shimmery, sheer white fabric with a high, straight neckline, wrist-length sleeves, and a long skirt. By a trick of the light playing on the two layers of fabric, it looked opaque, and very demure, but at moments, with certain movements, it became almost fully transparent. Her warm mocha skin glowed through the fabric, and underneath she was wearing only a skin-coloured thong.

Dana smiled and put her hand on the arm Sir Henry offered, stepping down into the bar at his side as people gazed entranced. "Kamila," she told him in an under-voice. "A new designer launching here in the autumn. She says this dress is going to make her name."

Dana's black hair, long and thick, fell like a cloak around her shoulders and down her back. Her makeup was expertly applied to enhance her dark, heavy-lashed eyes and high, strong cheekbones. She wore delicate tan-coloured sandals and carried a tiny bag.

"On anyone but yourself it would be a dismal failure, but she is perfectly right. Every woman in this room will be knocking on her door tomorrow, foolishly hoping to be made to look like you."

Dana was five foot eleven with a perfect figure, curved and long, with high breasts, athletic legs, and a firm musculature. Her smoky skin usually meant that as an actress she was cast in "ethnic" roles—whether First Nation rebel, exotic outworlder, or Arab princess. Or her current soap role—Reena, the bitchy, repressed, high-flying South Asian lawyer.

"Would you like some bubbly, Dana?" Sir Henry asked, neatly whisking a glass of champagne from a waiter's tray and offering it to her. "Not for me, dear boy, my heart, you know," he added, waving one pale hand with studied elegance. "Do you think you could find me a scotch?—double, no water."

"Oh, yes, Sir John! Of course!" said the waiter, enthusiastically if inaccurately, and headed for the long bar, behind which men and women in black and white bustled to provide for the guests of the charity function.

"They are so young these days," Sir Henry complained mildly. "They don't show my Lear in the schools anymore, of course."

"I don't think they teach *King Lear* at all," Dana sympathized. "Not accessible enough, Shakespeare."

A man was staring at her from across the room. The whole room was manoeuvring, overtly or covertly, to get a look at the dress; she had been prepared for that. But this man was different. He looked disapproving. Dana flicked a careless eyebrow at him and turned her attention back to "the best Lear the world has seen this century."

"Ah, the new barbarians," he was saying. "And why are you here tonight, my dear, giving a view of your body to the masses? A particular interest in Bagestani Drought Relief, or merely part of the general celebrity sweep? I understand they've pulled out all the stops for this one." He glanced around the crowd with studied disdain. His mouth worked thoughtfully. "Too far, perhaps."

She laughed, as she was meant to. "A little of both. They did scoop the cast of *Brick Lane,* but I would probably have been targeted anyway—I'm half Bagestani, Sir Henry."

She glanced at the disapproving man again: he had a dark intensity that made him magnetic. She was annoyed by the compulsion, but couldn't resist it. For a moment their eyes met. Then, dismissing her, he dropped his gaze to someone who was speaking to him.

Who the hell did he think he was? Dana looked him over. He was wearing a dark red, matte silk, Eastern-cut jacket over ivory silk *shalwar* trousers, and some pretty impressive jewellery, as well as what looked like war medals. He also seemed to have a chain of office. Although by his looks he might be a Bagestani, no representative of the Ghasib regime would be at this function.

"Really?" Sir Henry replied, his eyebrows raised. "I was under the impression that you were Ojibwa—was that just studio publicity?"

Dana had played the small part of a First Nation woman brought to England from Canada during the early nineteenth century in a film in which Sir Henry had had the starring role.

"My mother's Ojibwa, my father Bagestani," she said shortly. She glanced around the room. People were still nudging each other and talking about her dress, but the dark man was now apparently unaware of her existence. "Usually they play up whatever side suits the publicity machine."

"Yes, of course," he said, eyeing her up and down. "Astonishing how beautifully some races mix. Makes one wonder why the great prejudice grew up against interracial marriage. I am sure we—"

"Sir Henry," Dana said abruptly, "that tall man over there was looking at you. Do you know him?"

He turned his head absently. "If a man was looking this way, my dear, and I am sure they all are, he—oh, good evening, Dickie," he interrupted himself as an actor of his generation accosted him. "Still kicking, then. Do you know Dana Morningstar?"

On Dana's other side a woman took advantage of the interruption to approach her and claim her attention.

"I have to confess that I watch *Brick Lane* regularly! And I think the show is going to be absolutely *destroyed* without Reena. I love you in that—you are so cool and bitchy, you never let Jonathan get away with it!" she enthused. "Everyone I know was *so* upset to hear you were being written out!"

Dana smiled with the charm that always made people comment on how different she was from bitchy Reena, and murmured politely.

"No, it's absolutely true! You make that show!" the woman overrode her, much more interested in her own voice than her idol's. "Do you know yet how it's going to happen to Reena? Is it going to be murder or anything like that?"

Dana had done her final day of filming last week, but—"I'm sworn to secrecy, I'm afraid," she apologized with a smile.

She heard much more in the same vein as the next hour progressed. For an hour the celebrities, major and minor, were rubbing shoulders in the bar with the paying guests, who had parted with substantial sums of money for the privilege, and would be parted from more during the course of the evening.

A magazine photographer's assistant was working his way through the crowd asking the celebrities, two at a time, to go and pose for shots under the special lighting that had been set up in one corner. A photographer from a newspaper was walking around the room taking candid shots.

Sometimes she thought she felt the man's gaze brushing her again, but when she glanced over she never caught him looking her way. Maybe she was imagining it. She irritably rejected the idea as soon as she thought of it—he was the last man in the world she would obsess over. She knew what he was like without exchanging one word with him.

She was sure that if she asked anyone about him he would notice, and she was determined not to give him the satisfaction. He was certainly on the "celebrity" side: women were drooling over him with the special fixity reserved for men who are rich, handsome, young *and* famous all together.

Not that he was all that handsome, Dana told herself critically, watching as he dutifully took his turn posing for the photographer. His face was composed of angles too strong and stern for handsomeness. There was too much strength in the set of his jaw, the discipline of the wide mouth. He had square, thick black eyebrows over black eyes that seemed to set icy fire to whatever they touched. He was slim and spare, his shoulders square under his jacket. There seemed to be a weight of responsibility on him, and she could only guess his age at between twenty-five and forty.

She didn't like him. She didn't like him at all.

But it occurred to her that she always knew exactly where he was in the room. Of course it was only because she was the tallest woman in the room and he was at least six-two, but still…

"Ladies and gentlemen, in a moment we'll be moving into the ballroom," one of the organizers announced, and she surfaced and realized that she had spent the past five minutes in a daze, with no idea what she had said or what had been said to her. "If you don't yet know your table, please check the charts by the entrance."

"Have you found yours yet, Dana?"

Jenny, the actress who played her roommate, Desirée, on the show, was at her elbow.

"Clueless," Dana replied cheerfully, as they kissed cheeks.

"I'm sure you'll be at Table G with the rest of us." The two women linked arms and moved towards the crowd around the chart beside the wide entrance to the ballroom.

"That dress is going to cause a riot, Dana," Jenny murmured, completely without envy. She was Dana's opposite in nearly every physical feature—she was a curly-headed blond, with a round, cheerful, motherly face and a short dumpy shape. But she was fun, loyal and a good friend, as well as an excellent actress, and she never seemed to envy anyone anything.

Dana laughed. "Is it shocking?"

"You have no idea, my pet! You turn your head or lift an arm and suddenly you're naked! I've seen more than one spilled drink!"

"Well, that's the idea," Dana observed. "It's supposed to get me noticed."

"And who is that broody alpha male you're carefully not exchanging glances with?"

Dana's cheeks got warm. "Who do you mean?"

Jenny laughed and squeezed her arm. "You know very well who I mean. First he looks at you, then you look at him, and you're both careful never to be caught at it. Darling, have you had a complicated affair with a handsome sheikh and managed to keep it secret?"

Dana jerked upright. "I don't even know his name, and I certainly don't want to learn it! Where did you get the idea I knew him?"

"Oh...just a certain sizzle in the air," Jenny said,

mock dreamily. "The air between you is distorted, sort of like when heat is rising over the desert sands...."

A man with a clipboard stopped them before Dana could argue.

"It's quite all right, I can check for you, Miss Morningstar!" he said, so obviously smitten that Jenny laughed. He riffled through his pages. "Table D," he announced. "That's about five o'clock on the inner circle if you take the dais as twelve."

This cryptic comment made sense a few moments later when they moved into the ballroom. Against the centre of the back wall was a raised octagonal dais where a Middle Eastern ensemble, including the traditional *tar, setar, nay* and *santur,* as well as zither and violin, was tuning up. Around the dais was a polished octagonal dance floor, and around that were arranged tiers of round tables, each seating eight people.

The band began playing as the guests entered and spread out to find their tables—a haunting melody that Dana recognized. It was a traditional Bagestani song called *Aina al Warda?*—"Where is the Rose?"—which had taken on a special resonance for the expatriate Bagestanis, all so bitterly opposed to Ghasib's terrible regime. Her father had played it to Dana and her sister throughout her childhood.

"I wonder why you're not at Table G with the rest of us?" Jenny moaned after accompanying her to Table D and discovering, contrary to both inclination and expectation, that the man with the clipboard was right.

"It's a bore," Dana agreed, but there wasn't going to be a seating change now.

"Who are you with, then?" Jenny bent to the cards on either side of Dana's own. The band was giving *Aina al Warda?* all it had, and as people around the room sank into their seats, Dana saw another stern dark man looking her way. He was dressed in the Western style, black tie, and looked as though he was wondering whether to cross over to her.

Her father.

Where is the Rose?
When will I see her?
The nightingale asks after his beloved....

She stared at him. Well, this put a whole new complexion on the fund-raising evening. This was no mere Drought Relief Campaign. Her father would not have come to any ordinary charity fund-raiser for Bagestan. He was convinced that, in spite of everyone's best efforts, most of the money raised in good faith in the West went straight into President Ghasib's own coffers and the poor scarcely saw a penny.

Dana took a fresh look around at the other guests. They were top bracket; the tickets to this affair had been very pricey. Only about half of them were the usual run of charity supporters and celebrity hunters, though.

The other half were wealthy, educated Bagestani expats—mostly those of a certain age who had been rich enough to get out of the country in sixty-nine, but sprinkled with a few who had come as refugees in the years since and made good. The next generation, the foreign-born sons and daughters like herself, were also well represented.

The women were mostly in traditional Bagestani dress of beautifully decorated *shalwar kamees* and trailing gold-embroidered scarf, and a number of the older men were in immaculate white djellabas. More than one of them, hearing that music, now had eyes that were brighter for tears.

Her father was still looking at her. She wondered if he had seen her dress. She hoped so. She was suddenly filled with a dry, dead fury, as if her father had somehow manipulated her presence here. Logic told her that was impossible.

"Hellooo," Jenny carolled.

Dana surfaced, nodded a cool acknowledgement to her father and turned away. "Sorry, what did you say?"

"Sir John Cross," Jenny repeated, pointing to the card at the place setting to one side of Dana's. "Who's he?"

"A diplomat, I think. Or, he was." She had a vague memory of her father's voice. "Wasn't he the British Ambassador to Bagestan at the time of the coup?"

"Search me!" Jenny shrugged. "Poor Dana! And Sheikh Ashraf Durran," she read from the card on her other side. "One of those boring old farts in white skirts, I bet. My poor darling, it's going to be a long night for you."

"It is going to be a very successful fund-raising night," Dana told her with dry sarcasm, unable to hold down her irritation.

"Is it? How do you know?" Jenny asked with a smile. She wasn't big on world affairs, Dana reminded herself. And her interest in such things as mind manipulation techniques began and ended with using her disarming, housewifely smile in fabric softener commercials.

"Because it may say Drought Relief on the banners, but the real story behind this little event is Line Our Pockets with Gold and One Day We'll Restore the Monarchy in Bagestan!" she told Jenny through her teeth. "God, these people make me sick!"

Jenny blinked. "What do—"

"Listen to that music! They're deliberately playing on everyone's insane hopes for Ghasib to be overthrown and a new sultan to come riding in on his white horse and turn back the clock to the Golden Age! It's not going to happen, but they will get a fortune from the deluded tonight! It's unspeakable!"

Jenny was looking at her in surprise. Dana wasn't often like this, except when she was on the set playing the overexcitable Reena.

"But, Dana, wouldn't you rather see Ghasib kicked out? Wouldn't it be a good thing if one of the al Whatsit princes could be found and restored to the throne?"

"You've been reading the Sunday papers, Jenny. It's nothing but ink and hot air. There *are* no al Jawadi princes! Ghasib had them all assassinated years ago. If anybody kicks Ghasib out, it is going to be the Islamic militants, and that's just going to be a case of out of the frying pan, isn't it?"

"But what about that one in *Hello!* magazine a couple of weeks back, who had amnesia? He was *so* gorgeous, too. He's a grandson of the old sultan, and it said—"

"Najib al Makhtoum is not a viable candidate for the throne, even if he is who they say he is, which I doubt. They are all completely deluded, these people, and somebody is making sure they stay deluded." She belatedly noticed the alarm in Jenny's eyes, heaved a sigh and smiled.

"Sorry, Jen, but I got this stuff all my life from my father, and I hate it. You're right, they are a bunch of boring old farts who want their palaces and oil rigs back and can't accept that it isn't going to happen. God, I wish I hadn't come! It might be tolerable if I were sitting with you and the others. This way—" she gestured at the label that read *Sheikh Ashraf Durran* "—in addition to everything else, I'll have to listen to a whole lot of demented ravings about how we've got Ghasib on the ropes at last.''

''Never mind,'' Jenny murmured mock-placatingly, ''you can always marry him. He's probably got lots of money, and that's what really matters.''

''Not if he were the last sheikh on the planet!'' Dana vowed.

Jenny laughed, leaned to kiss Dana's cheek again and moved off. Dana turned her head—and found herself looking at the harsh-faced stranger from a distance of a few feet. By the look on his face, not only was he an al Jawadi supporter, he had overheard every word of their conversation.

Two

For a moment she thought he was going to pass on by, but he stopped and faced her. His eyes bored into hers, but against a little shiver of feeling she couldn't define, she managed to hold her gaze steady.

"Are you an optimist, Miss Golbahn, or a pessimist?" he asked in conversational tones.

Typical of a man like him to call her by her father's, not her professional name. She was quite sure it was deliberately calculated.

"Don't you mean, am I a dreamer or a realist?"

"No, I don't mean that," he replied, in a careful tone that infuriated her. His eyebrows moved expressively. "I mean, when you say that the restoration of the monarchy is impossible, do you speak from your wishes, or your fears?"

He had absolutely no right to challenge her about a

conversation he had eavesdropped on in the first place. His arrogance made her grit her teeth—and tell a lie.

"I have no wishes one way or the other. I am simply calling it as I see it."

"You have no wish to see a vicious dictator who destroys his country and his people swept from power," he repeated, his face hardening.

She was damned if she would retract now.

"What good would my hopes do anyone?"

His burning gaze flicked down over her body, then back up to her face again. She suddenly felt what a disadvantage it was not to know whether she was naked or not. Had he just looked at her breasts?

"Do you feel you owe nothing to your father, Miss Golbahn?" he asked.

She stared at him in open-mouthed, indignant astonishment. Typical of a man like him to imagine a twenty-six-year-old woman should govern her actions according to her father's pride!

"Who *do* you think you're talking to?" she demanded, dimly realizing that heads were now turning in their direction.

"I—"

"My name is Morningstar," she overrode him in her coldest voice. "And how accounts stand between me and my father is absolutely none of your business."

His eyes narrowed at her, but if he expected her to be cowed, he could think again. She tilted her chin and gave him stare for stare. Her tone was no more insulting than his own had been, and she would be quite happy to point that out to him. But the man bowed his head a fraction.

"I apologize. I was given to understand that you were Colonel Golbahn's daughter."

"My father is Khaldun Golbahn. He is no longer a

colonel, and the regiment he was colonel of hasn't existed for over thirty years," she returned through her teeth.

Before he could respond to this, a waiter appeared to pull out her chair, and Dana gratefully turned away and sank down to accept a napkin on her lap. Only a few people were still milling around, tying up their conversations before heading to separate tables. People were watching her more or less covertly, and she realized that her argument with the stranger had given them another reason to stare and whisper.

She could sense that he was still hovering behind her. She hoped he wasn't intending to get in the last word. Dana picked up the printed menu card propped in front of her wineglass and wished he would disappear.

"Sheikh Durran!" a crusty old voice exclaimed with satisfaction.

"Sir John," his voice replied, and she almost fainted with horror. Her eyes flew to the place card at the setting next to her. *Sheikh Ashraf Durran.*

Ya Allah, she would be sitting beside him for the next two hours!

The two men were shaking hands behind her, and she heard the clap of hand against shoulder. "I was hoping to see you." The old man dropped his voice. "How did your brother manage? Can I assume your presence tonight means I am to congratulate you?"

Dana found she was holding her breath. There was an air of mystery over the conversation, suddenly, and it gripped her. She bent further over the menu card, but she wasn't taking in one word of what was printed.

"He was successful, Sir John, in a manner of speaking—and flying by the seat of his pants, as usual."

He spoke quietly. His voice now held a hint of humour that she hadn't been privileged to hear when he spoke to her. It was deep and strong, as compelling as the man. A voice an actor would kill for.

"You have it safe, then?" The old man was whispering now.

"I do."

"Tremendous! Well done, all of you! One might almost say, an omen."

"Mash'Allah."

The two men sat, one on either side of her. Dana stared fixedly at the menu. She had never felt so unnerved by a situation. She reminded herself how many times in the past she had made conversation with awkward, difficult strangers, more or less successfully. There was no reason to feel as though there was a chasm in front of her.

Waiters were already circulating with trays of starters and pouring wine. Onstage the *tar* was being played with a heartrending virtuosity that no other instrument, she thought, ever achieved.

"Asparagus or tabbouleh?" the waiter asked her.

Dana loved the food of Bagestan; she had been raised on it. At sixteen she had stopped eating it, as a rejection of her father and all he stood for. That time of rebellion was long past; she was twenty-six now. But she found herself thrown back into that old, combative mind-set now.

She wanted to let Sheikh Ashraf Durran know that she was not to be judged by any of his rules. As she had her father.

"Asparagus, thank you," she said, and a plate of butter-soaked green spears was set before her. She took a sip of wine.

"Tabbouleh," Sheikh Durran firmly requested a moment later. She noticed that there was no wine in his wineglass. Well, she could have guessed that.

In the loud buzz of conversation that was going up all around the ballroom, it seemed to her that the silence between the two of them must be as obvious to everyone as their earlier disagreement. She wondered if gossip about them would find its way into the tabloids. Journalists often needed no more. Find a button and sew a coat onto it was their motto.

Dana glanced around the table in the hopes of finding a conversation to join. Somehow she had got put in with the political crowd. She recognized an academic who was often called in to discuss Bagestani affairs on a BBC current events program, and a television journalist who had made her name covering the Parvan-Kaljuk War and whose career was now devoted to reporting from one Middle East hot spot or another. Dana thought she would have enjoyed talking to them. But they were directly across the table from her, chatting quietly together.

Sir John Cross, too, was engaged with the person on his other side.

"You have no desire to see your father restored to his command, Miss Morningstar?" Sheikh Durran clearly had no reservations about picking up where they had left off.

Dana picked up a stalk of asparagus and turned her head. Up close she recognized the Parvan flag on one of his medals. He was a veteran of the Parvan-Kaljuk War, then, but she was no closer to knowing who he was.

"I have no *expectation* of seeing it," she returned, before biting into the tender, delicious tip.

"Why not?"

"My father is, after all, nearly sixty. Not very much younger than President Ghasib." She said the name deliberately, for in expat circles it wasn't the thing to give the dictator his title. Saying it on an occasion like this was tantamount to declaring herself on the Ghasib side.

She wasn't on the Ghasib side and never had been, not even in her days of wildest rebellion. But no way was she going to fall meekly in line with the sheikh's expectations.

She pushed the buttery stalk into her mouth. There was no change in the sheikh's expression, but suddenly she felt the phallic symbolism of it, almost as if he had pointed it out to her. *Dream on!* she wanted to snap. She chewed, then licked the butter from her fingertips before deliberately reaching for her wine again.

Sheikh Durran seemed to take no notice. He picked up a small lettuce leaf and used it to pinch up some of his tabbouleh salad.

"Do you think the only thing that will remove Ghasib from power is death from old age?"

She chose another stalk. She opened her mouth, wondering if she could unnerve him by sucking the butter from the tip. Her eyes flicked to his. His look was dry and challenging, and without any warning, heat flamed in her cheeks.

"Even granting the unlikely proposition that there was an al Jawadi heir," she said defiantly, "even granting that this mysterious person should at last reveal himself and, even more amazingly, make the risky attempt to take power, and then granting that he should be successful in restoring the monarchy in Bagestan—what are the odds that my father would be given his old job back by someone who wasn't even born at the time he held it?"

His eyebrows went up, but he made no answer.

"But the truth, if people would stop being excited by

newspaper reports as reliable as sightings of the Abominable Snowman, is that it's a mirage. No prince is going to come riding in on his white horse and wave his magic wand to make Ghasib disappear.''

''You know this?''

''Look—I got that nostalgia stuff at my daddy's knee. He talked of nothing else all through my childhood. When I was a kid, I believed it. I had a huge crush on the mysterious Crown Prince who was going to make it all happen. I wrote letters to him. I even had a dream that I was going to marry him when I grew up. But he never came, did he? Thirty years now.

''I paid my dues, Sheikh Durran. I believed the myth as firmly as I believed in Santa Claus. After my mother and father split Santa Claus never visited our house again, but I went on believing in him. And I went on believing in the al Jawadi restoration, too. But a dream like that only lasts so long. And then one day you wake up and realize—it's a fairy tale.''

''And at what age did you wake up?''

Dana tensed and wished she hadn't spoken so openly. She wasn't sure why she had. ''From the Santa Claus myth, eight. From the prince on a white horse fiction, sixteen,'' she said shortly, and applied herself to her meal.

''Sixteen,'' Sheikh Ashraf repeated consideringly. ''That's young to stop believing in justice.''

She supposed he was right. But she had had a very rude and sudden awakening.

Dana shrugged, demolished another spear of asparagus, and wiped her fingers on her napkin. He waited, and she felt forced to answer. She waved a hand at the room.

''What amazes me is the number of people who never wake up—who refuse to wake up.''

''What happened at sixteen that took the stars from your eyes?''

I discovered that the father I adored was a monster and nothing he said was to be believed.

She shrugged and lied again. ''Nothing in particular.''

His gaze probed her for an uncomfortable moment, but to her relief he let it pass.

''And what happened to your letters?'' he asked.

''What?'' she asked blankly. She automatically leaned towards him as the waiter cleared her plate.

''The letters you wrote to the Crown Prince. What became of them?''

She really wished she hadn't told him about that. It wasn't a part of her past she confided very often. Something had knocked her off her centre tonight.

''I really don't know.'' Her tone said, *don't care.*

''They were never sent?''

''Where to? My father told me Crown Prince Kamil had escaped from the palace as a baby, with his mother carrying him in a load of Ghasib's dirty laundry. He said they got to Parvan, but no one knew any more than that, did they?''

He hesitated. ''Some knew more.''

She wasn't sure what made her ask, ''Did you ever meet him?''

Again he hesitated. ''Yes, I met him.''

''He died fighting in the Kaljuk War, didn't he? Is that where you knew him?''

Sheikh Ashraf turned his head and lifted a hand as the waiter started to fill his glass with wine. ''No, thank you.''

When he turned back he seemed to have forgotten her

question. After a moment Dana nodded towards the row of medals on his chest.

"You were in the Kaljuk War?"

His eyelids came down as he nodded.

"Are you Parvani?" He didn't sound it.

"I was born in Barakat," he said. "I was in Prince Omar's Company."

The almost legendary Company of Cup Companions, led by Prince Omar of Central Barakat, who had gone to war on Prince Kavian's side. She had followed their fortunes while still at drama school. All her friends had had crushes on the Cup Companions and had plagued Dana with questions, feeling sure that, because of her background, she knew more than they did.

And she had, a little. At least she knew what the term Cup Companion meant. "In the old days, it used to mean the guys the king went on the prowl with. The sons of the aristocracy. They weren't supposed to know or care about politics or government, only wine and love and poetry." Cue for sighs. "But nowadays it's just the opposite. They're the prince's special advisors and stuff like that. By tradition he has twelve of them," she had explained.

There had been many more than the twelve in the Company, of course. Others recruited had been made Honorary Companions. So it wasn't foolish to ask, "Are you one of his Cup Companions?"

He replied with a little nod. She should have guessed before. But she'd forgotten until now that Cup Companions from Parvan and the Barakat Emirates were supposed to be attending tonight.

"What's your interest in the al Jawadis?" she pressed.

He eyed her consideringly for a moment. "Prince

Omar is related to the al Jawadi through the Durrani. I, too, am a Durrani.''

"And you want to help the al Jawadi back to the throne?''

His raised his eyebrows. "Tonight we are here to raise money not for the al Jawadi, but for the victims of the drought which Ghasib's insane agricultural policies have created.''

"Maybe, on the surface, but you know and I know that tonight there are going to be lots of under-the-table donations to the al Jawadi campaign as well.''

"Do we?''

The waiter had refilled her wineglass and she took another sip. There was juice on the table for non-drinkers, but she noticed Sheikh Durran stuck to water. But refusing alcohol didn't prove he was a good man. No doubt her father was doing the same.

"Born in Barakat, you said. Are you Bagestani by blood?'' Not all the refugees from Ghasib's regime had fled to England or Canada, by any means. More had gone to Parvan and Barakat.

"I am half Barakati, half Bagestani,'' he said, after a pause in which he seemed to calculate.

"Ah! So you're one of those who never stopped believing in the fairy tale?''

His lips twitched again. "You might say that. And you, Miss Morningstar—you do not believe anyone is capable of removing Ghasib from power?''

"Salmon or chicken?'' the waiter interrupted, and quickly set down what she asked for.

She chose automatically and scarcely noticed the interruption.

"Well, there's always the possibility that another ambitious nephew may one day be successful in some renewed assassination attempt, I suppose,'' she allowed, helping herself to the beautifully cooked vegetables offered. ''Or the Islamic militants may pull it off. But Ghasib does seem to deal with both those possibilities in a very convincing way, doesn't he? I can't help feeling that anyone with their eyes on power, even a prince, if there is one, might be content to wait until natural causes win the day for them.''

He concentrated on the vegetables for a moment. ''You think the fear of death makes cowards of us all?''

His part of the conversation so far seemed to consist entirely of questions. ''Maybe. It's the undiscovered country, isn't it? 'Thus conscience doth make cowards of us all,''' she recited.

His mouth went up on one side. It was the first smile she had had from him. ''And who said that?''

''Hamlet. Isn't that who you were paraphrasing?''

This produced a small laugh. Humour transformed him, she found. The fire in his eyes turned to sparkle, and he suddenly seemed much younger. Now she would place him at well under thirty-five.

''I was not paraphrasing anyone.'' The flow to the new conversation was seamless as he pursued, ''You know the play well?''

''I starred in a school production.''

''Interesting—I thought the star part was Hamlet himself.''

''It is the star part.'' She grinned, but still did not feel easy with him. ''I was at a girls' school.''

''And you were the tallest girl?''

It occurred to her suddenly that he did not know who she was. That was why he had called her by her father's name. Well, no surprise if a man like him didn't watch the soaps, and she hadn't yet landed a major film part.

She laughed. What did it matter? "Yes, I was the tallest girl by a long way," she said. "I was a natural for the part."

Three

"**G**ood evening, ladies and gentlemen."

Dana and Sheikh Ashraf had chatted more amiably for a few minutes, and then, mercifully, the conversation had opened up and become general around the table. Now the meal, delicious by any standards and stupendous compared to the food served at most other charity functions she had attended, was finished. Coffee and liqueurs had been served.

Now it was down to business.

"We have a wonderful evening lined up for you tonight...."

Dana absently sipped her Turkish coffee and let the voice of the master of ceremonies wash over her. The organizer was introduced, an earnest, small man talking about the drought and the famine it had caused. And, knowing his audience, making much of President

Ghasib's deliberate mismanagement of Bagestan's agriculture and his habit of pocketing charity funds.

"But we have negotiated with Ghasib's government to put our own representatives on the ground in Bagestan, and management of the funds raised tonight will never leave our control until it is safe in the hands of those who need it most...."

"I wonder if that's true," Dana murmured.

"Very difficult to manage, I should have thought," Sir John Cross agreed in a low voice. "However, what else can one do? I think we must assume that some of the money gets through to those who actually need it."

"And while we may hope and believe that we're getting closer by the day to the moment when Ghasib's government will be history, our priority toni—"

The audience interrupted him with applause. Dana shook her head and glanced towards Sheikh Ashraf. He was looking very sober, leaning back in his chair, his arms crossed. He was not applauding.

He turned his head and caught her eye with a dark, level gaze that seemed to probe and assess, and made her heart pound, but what he had gleaned from the examination, she couldn't guess.

The organizer wisely kept it short and then the real star of the evening took the mike. Roddy Evans was a well-known and popular comedian, always in demand for events like this because of his ability to put people into a generous, good-natured mood and then get bundles of money out of them. Dana had always liked him.

"All right, I want every table to elect a captain, please!" he said, when his warm-up had reduced everyone to cheers, laughter and applause. "Just choose one person who'll keep the rest of you in line this evening and take money from your wallets when instructed to do so...."

"I think it better be Dana!" someone announced. "If it comes to delivering money to the stage, she's the one they'll all want to see," and the rest of the table quickly agreed.

"Sheikh Durran looks like a much better bet," Dana protested, more out of curiosity to see how he would react than anything else. "He's at least big enough to make any threat stick."

"But one catches more flies with honey," he said smoothly, waving a hand, and they all laughed and agreed.

Dana gave in with a threat.

"You'll be sorry. Be afraid, be very afraid. I will *soak* you."

Being captain turned out to be a not very onerous duty. At intervals throughout the evening, on instruction, Dana had to get a five- or ten-pound note from each of the people seated at her table and pass the money on to one of the roving hostesses. Most people were familiar with the format and had come with a supply of folding money as well as their chequebooks. In the meantime there was plenty of nonsense to keep people laughing and donating.

After a while came what most of the paying guests considered the high point—the auction. Tonight there were some real prizes. Top of the list was an all-expense-paid first-class two-week holiday at the Hotel Sheikh Daud in West Barakat, sponsored by Prince Karim.

But that would come near the end, as would the brand-new Subaru donated by Ahmed Bashir Motors. Before that there was some very exciting and somewhat drink-inspired bidding for weekends at country hotels, meals in restaurants, books, celebrity memorabilia, theatre tickets—whatever the organizers had been able to screw out of donors. The organizers here had clearly been top rank, and there was a stream of the kind of prizes that were often the top prize at lesser events.

Sprinkled among them were half a dozen "personal appearance" donations. Certain celebrities had agreed to spend an evening at a restaurant with whoever bid the highest for the honour. In the ruthless way of the entertainment industry, these prizes, like the others, were graded according to ascending value through the evening, because of the excitement the increasing amounts of money generated from the guests.

It was always interesting, and often salutary for those concerned, to see which celebrities were expected to bring in only a low bid, and which were saved to the end—with the other best prizes. The celebrities usually hated the whole process.

Most of such celebrities were women, and tonight all were, which Dana supposed was a comment on the way society was still run. She was always asked to participate in such an auction, and sometimes did, though always disliking it. If a man got you for too little, he treated you with contempt. If he paid a lot, often he thought he should be able to expect a little more than your face over the dinner table. Or, worst of all, he invited a whole horde of his friends along and expected you to act as his hostess for the evening.

But good charity organizers were ruthless, and this one had been prime, and Dana had given in.

Her name hadn't been called yet. This was making her nervous, because although the early names didn't usually get up in front of the crowd during the auction, the later names were often asked to do so. This let you in for even more potential humiliation if your drawing power wasn't as strong as the organizers had assumed.

Jenny's name had come up early. She stayed in her seat, but she had got a very respectable two thousand pounds from a real estate agent whose company name was called out at least eight times during the prolonged bidding by the savvy Roddy. Dana had expected to be the next celebrity auctioned after an interval of theatre tickets and a year's membership to a top gym, but she wasn't.

Nor was she the next, nor the next.

She began to feel really uncomfortable. She was not a movie star, after all; they were the ones who pulled in the really big sums. She was a mere soap star with only a couple of film credits, and if she went up after high bids and scored much less than the previous celeb, it would be embarrassing.

Next up was a gorgeous, big-breasted but brain-dead television presenter, who was called up onstage for the auction and who, after a long and well-hyped bidding war between a Harley Street cosmetic surgeon and a new car dealer, pulled nearly five thousand pounds. It was a figure which impressed the whole room.

A set of golf clubs came next, but it was clear all the real emotional heat this time had become focussed on the human portion of the auction. A very well-known middle-aged movie actress who had been included in last year's Honours List and was now a Dame raised just over six thousand pounds. Dana started to feel very uncomfortable. Why had this woman been listed before her? It was ridiculous. Dana didn't have anything like her pulling power.

Maybe Dana's name had just been forgotten by the organizer. She certainly hoped so.

"It's a bit like a slave auction," the journalist across the table observed dispassionately, making Dana cringe even more. "I wonder why they do it?"

"Because we are made to feel, by whoever is pressuring us, that it is a small thing to ask and everyone else has agreed and we are selfish and smug if we refuse," Dana said clearly.

And just then Roddy cried, "...a dinner date at the fabulous Riverfront Restaurant with our very own favourite bitch, Reena! Otherwise known as *Brick Lane* star *Dana Morningstar!* And she's here tonight, ladies and gentlemen, so will you come up here, Reena, I mean, Dana, and let the folks take a look at the merchandise?"

Dana lifted her eyebrows at the journalist as one of the ever-present assistants dashed in to hold her chair and escort her to the stage amid an enthusiastic round of applause and cheers.

She smiled and twinkled her fingers as she stepped up under the lights, and wondered whether her dress was opaque or transparent at the moment.

"...and together you'll dine on caviar, lobster and champagne provided by the fabulous Riverfront Restaurant, which as you all know is one of London's most fabulous eateries! It's moored right on the Thames, and you'll be driven home afterwards in a chauffeur-driven Rolls-Royce provided by Launcelot Limos!

"So now, what am I bid for a delightful evening in Dana Morningstar's company? You might even learn from her the secret of Reena's demise before it's broadcast! Do I hear five hundred, ladies and gentlemen?"

"Five hundred!"

"Oooh, quick off the mark there, Harold. That's Harold McIntosh, ladies and gentlemen, not short of a bob or two when you run a Mayfair car dealership, now, are you? Five hundred, do I hear—''

''One thousand!''

''Ah, ha! Well, this promises to be a very exciting auction, ladies and gentlemen, not reticent at all, are we? That's a thousand bid from—''

''Ten thousand pounds.''

It wasn't a shout, but somehow the voice cut through the chatter and was heard by everyone. There was a collective gasp all over the room. Not only because of the enormous leap in the bidding, but because of the quality of the voice. Firm, assured, brooking no interference. And not at all the worse for drink.

Sheikh Ashraf Durrani's voice.

Dana felt her cheeks flame. She bit her lip. She had never had to work so hard to force a smile in her life, but she managed it. She even managed to fake a little wide-eyed, excited grimace.

''Ten thousand pounds, ladies and gentlemen! Well, now we're getting serious. And who is going to take that higher, I wonder? Jeremy, accountant to the stars, you're in this league, do I hear a raise on ten thousand for an evening with Dana Gorgeous Morningstar? What about you, George—''

''Ten thousand one hundred!'' cried a slightly inebriated voice.

''Ah ha! We're really cooking with—''

''Fifteen thousand pounds.''

It was the sheikh again, speaking as flatly as if he were giving an underling an order. The skin on Dana's body shivered into goose bumps. He was making it so obvious.

''Well, well, Sheikh Durran! I see you're pretty determined to get what you want. Do I hear any bids over fifteen thousand?'' cried Roddy, just a little nonplussed, because it suddenly was difficult to inject the humour and good-natured ribaldry he was such at expert at into the proceedings. The room was filled with an excited buzz. Dana, standing in a bright spot, just kept smiling.

It was a struggle. What on earth did the man think he was doing? To be the highest bidder was one thing. To carry on like this meant everyone would be talking! They'd be the subject of endless speculation, and the story would probably make it into the tabloids. They'd never get any peace if they appeared in public.

And yet part of her couldn't resist the lure of being thought so attractive. Fifteen thousand pounds in a couple of minutes! And such a powerful, influential man! It was like a fairy tale.

She saw Jenny and the others at the *Brick Lane* table gazing at her in blank, slightly reproachful astonishment, as if a secret part of her life had been revealed and they felt they should have known about it.

''...and gone! To Sheikh Ashraf Durran. I'm told you're one of Prince Omar of Central Barakat's most trusted advisors, Sheikh Durran, and I'm sure he'll agree you've shown excellent judgement tonight!''

The applause was thunderous as Dana was escorted back to her seat, a follow spot on her all the way.

''Whew!'' exclaimed Roddy, wiping the not-so-imaginary sweat from his brow. ''Ladies and gentlemen, what can we do to beat that? You'll have to work hard and bid high! And that won't be too difficult for our next prize—Prince Karim of West Barakat himself has actually donated this one, ladies and gentlemen. It's the one you've all been waiting for—well, except for a certain fairly obvious exception, who's already snaffled his prize! Here it is, a two-week holiday for two in the fabulous…''

''What on earth did you do that for?'' Dana hissed, as she sank into her chair. Everyone at the table was gazing at them in slightly stunned speculation. They must now believe one of two things—that Dana and the handsome sheikh already had a relationship, or that the sheikh was smitten and they were about to have one.

Nothing she could say was going to convince anyone otherwise, she was sure, but the moment she looked into his eyes she realized that it wasn't true. Whatever his reasons were, she knew damned well that Sheikh Ashraf Durran was anything but smitten with her. The expression in his eyes was anything but sexual interest.

A little seed of anger was born then.

He shrugged, and his next words confirmed her suspicions. ''Why not? That is what we are here for, to raise money.''

Inarguable. ''Well, after a display like that, I will not go out with you!'' she retorted childishly, in a low voice meant for his ears alone. ''We'd have every paparazzo in the city following us!''

He lifted his hands in a gesture that said it mattered not a jot whether she did or did not. ''Things are rarely what they promise to be. *Buyer Beware* I am sure is the first rule at such auctions.''

She could not get lighthearted about it. ''You have not bought me.''

He looked at her. ''No? But you were for sale, were you not? Or should we say for rent?''

That made her grit her teeth. ''I'll speak to the organizer, and you won't have to—''

He lifted a hand, cutting her off. ''Don't trouble, Miss Morningstar. I will not in any case be in the country beyond tomorrow. Take a friend and enjoy the lobster and the limousine without me.''

This made her even angrier, though she could dimly see that it shouldn't. She should have smiled graciously and said how generous he was and how the starving children in the Qermez Desert at least would benefit and that was what mattered. But she couldn't get the words past her teeth.

Maybe because she was gritting them.

''More coffee, Miss Morningstar?''

She was grateful for the excuse to turn her head. She nodded, and the waiter poured more sweet black sludge into her little cup. There was a plate of sugary Turkish delight which she had previously avoided, but now her irritation drove her to pick up a little cube. She bit it irritably in half. It was an unreal bright pink.

Meanwhile the holiday in Barakat was going for at least as much as it was probably worth.

She really couldn't have said why she was so irritated with him. To throw fifteen thousand pounds away like that—well, of course at first she had imagined it was because he was interested. And of course that had piqued her own interest. But why should she care if all he was interested in was making a show of his wealth while passing on money to charity?

The auction was over, but the wine was still flowing and there were more high jinks in store. People joined in with delight.

Not Dana. And not the stone-cold-sober Sheikh Ashraf. They stood up and sat down as instructed, and put their hands on their heads or their bums, and paraded around. But she noticed that when he turned out to be one of the group of men instructed to drop their trousers to their ankles and shuffle up onto the dance floor, he did not comply, and no one at the table even thought of challenging him on his dereliction.

But everybody else was having a marvellous time with all the nonsense, and the money was rolling in.

"Now, ladies and gentlemen, a little earlier in the evening, you were all handed out cards asking how much you would donate to Bagestan Drought Relief for the fun of a kiss. Yes? You were given the names of our six magic couples tonight—the men who bid for an evening with our lovely actress volunteers—and you voted for the couple you would most like to see kiss."

Dana felt a prickling of her skin, like a warning of doom. She flicked a glance at Sheikh Durran, and saw his mouth tighten. He knew, too. And was looking forward to it as much as she was.

"Now, while we've all been having such a fabulous good time, volunteers have been adding up all the votes and tallying them."

She had agreed to it—of course they wouldn't pull a thing like this without getting all the actresses' permission first. But she had agreed with a shrug, thinking it would be just one more thing. A one-in-six chance of having to kiss some smitten stranger in public—how bad could it be? No worse than the auction itself.

But it was going to be a whole lot worse.

"And ladies and gentlemen, at the risk of shattering some delicate egos, I can tell you, it was *no contest*. The pair you most want to see giving each other a kiss, ladies and gentlemen, is *Dana Morningstar and Sheikh Ashraf Durran!*"

The bright light of the follow spot fell on them. Sheikh Ashraf was sitting like a statue. Dana realized suddenly that *he* of course had not been consulted. For the sheikh this was coming totally out of left field.

And he liked it even less than she did. She knew that by his face. Sheikh Ashraf Durran looked like nothing so much as the masks of Hawk her Ojibwa grandfather carved.

But this was a pressure even the coldly disapproving sheikh would not be able to resist.

Four

"Now, first, I'm going to ask you all to put your money where your mouths are. Let's see how much you're willing to pay...."

Dana smiled. Sheikh Ashraf was still looking as though sparks would fly off if you hit him with a hammer.

She looked into his face and smiled deliberately at him. Everyone was watching. "It's inevitable," she murmured, her eyebrow giving a flirtatious flicker as if she were joking with him. "Let's just get it over with."

He hesitated. "We will look far less foolish if we give in gracefully," she warned him.

Meanwhile, Roddy was good-naturedly chivvying the audience into one last fit of generosity, reminding them of the starving children and the drought-stricken farms, making jokes about how poor old Sheikh Ashraf was going to have to kiss Dana, and what a terrible thing that was, while all the audience had to do was pay him to do it.

Someone drunkenly volunteered to stand in for the sheikh, and was speedily subdued by a witty rejoinder from Roddy that put off anyone else with that idea.

And the money buckets were going the rounds. At the edge of the stage someone was counting the cash and cheques and keeping Roddy advised as to the total.

Through it all the spotlight was on them. Dana smiled and laughed at the jokes. She no longer knew how Sheikh Ashraf was reacting, because although she smiled and flicked her eyes his way she didn't actually focus on him. Roddy was being decent, his patter was very lighthearted and without innuendo, and she didn't really understand why the whole thing was so hard to take.

Finally Roddy seemed to have milked them dry. He instructed the money-gatherers to pour all the money into a huge bucket at the front of the stage.

"Now, Dana, and Your Excellency, can I have you both up here on stage, please?"

Dana bit her lip and bent her head, taking a deep breath. Her blood was pounding in her head. She really didn't understand why. It was nothing. A quick kiss was all that was required. And yet...

She let the breath out on a sigh, lifted her head, and, as one of the waiters appeared behind her chair, prepared to stand.

A hand clamped on her arm, keeping her seated. Dana looked down stupidly, noting the strength in the square fingers that curled around her flesh, the tawny skin against the shimmery white fabric of her dress, the heat that burned through it.

"Wait here," he ordered softly.

He got to his feet, crossed the dance floor and moved

up onto the little stage. Such was his presence, his charisma, Dana noted with awe, that the rowdy audience fell immediately silent and expectant.

"You know me," he said, in his deep, firm voice. "You know who I am." She heard a gasp from a table behind her, and a murmur rustled through the room. He waited, looking around at the audience with the unsmiling, calm confidence of...she wasn't sure who she had ever seen with that kind of bone-deep authority.

The air seemed suddenly too heavy with expectation.

"I am Sheikh Ashraf Durran, Cup Companion to Prince Omar of Central Barakat. I am going to do what you want me to do, have no fear."

There was a massive roar of voices and applause, led, she saw, by the Bagestani contingent. He let it soar and peak, then cut it off with a raised hand.

"I am willing, even without your very generous donations." More cheers. "But this—" he gestured at the bucket of money at his feet with a flickering smile "—this is not by any means enough money to convince Miss Morningstar to make such a sacrifice as to kiss me."

She laughed along with everyone else. God, he should be a preacher! He was absolutely mesmerizing them! People began to shout and wave money and cheques, which the hostesses hurried to collect. Sheikh Durran stood with his arms folded, watching.

Roddy, she saw, was gazing at him in stunned admiration. He absently accepted a note passed to him by one of the hostesses, read it, then, with a glance at Sheikh Ashraf, put the mike to his lips.

"I have a note here from Ahmed Bashir of Ahmed Bashir Motors on the Edgware Road, pledging to double the amount raised! So come on, ladies and gentlemen, this is your chance to give double your money!"

Sheikh Ashraf looked and nodded towards the table where Ahmed Bashir was sitting, and another cheer went up. For a man who had started out looking as if he were carved in oak, he sure learned fast, Dana reflected.

"What does he do for Prince Omar?" someone at the table leaned to ask Dana.

It was a natural assumption, the way things had gone tonight. But there was too much noise for explanation, and she simply smiled and shook her head.

"Miss Morningstar," said Sheikh Ashraf from the stage, and Dana's head whipped around as if she were a puppet and he had caught her string. He put out a hand. In the room suddenly the sound of the air conditioning seemed loud.

"They give all this to the starving if you will kiss me, Dana. Do you agree?"

A waiter pulled out her chair. Dana got to her feet, feeling half hypnotized, and moved with swift grace towards him. Her heart was pounding, and the smile playing on her lips now was involuntary.

"Not everyone knows, I think, that Miss Morningstar herself has very close ties with Bagestan. Her father is Colonel Golbahn," said Sheikh Ashraf.

The Bagestanis in the audience were by now delirious. They screamed and cheered her up to the stage. Dana was totally bemused by the reaction.

"That is why—" They fell silent again, as if he held their strings, too. "That is why Miss Morningstar agrees to this blackmail. Because the money is going to a cause that is very close to all our hearts." Wild, almost hysterical applause. "The hungry, desperate children—all the hungry and desperate people—of Bagestan."

She reached the dais and lifted her hand. The platform was only a foot high, but Sheikh Ashraf seemed to tower over her. "You should take this kiss, therefore, as a symbol of our love for Bagestan, and our determination to fill the hungry ache of its people."

And with that he bent over her, wrapped his arms around her, lifted her bodily up against him, and clamped his mouth to hers with a passion and a thirst that made the world go black.

"You are *such* a sneak!" the voice carolled down the receiver.

Dana had answered the phone automatically, still half asleep. Now she rolled over and blinked at the clock. Seven thirty-eight. "Jenny, why are you calling at this hour?" she protested. Scraping her hair away from her ear, she punched a pillow into shape and slid up to a half sitting position in the bed.

"Oh, sorry, darling, I'm in Makeup! Are you in bed? I forgot how early it was," Jenny lied cheerfully.

"In a pig's eye," Dana muttered direfully.

"Is he there?" her friend hissed excitedly. "I really actually phoned thinking you wouldn't be home, to be honest."

"No, he is not here!" Dana told her indignantly. "Give me a break! I only met the man last night."

"Ha. That kiss had been building up steam for longer than a few hours. That kiss had History."

Dana shivered. "It didn't have steam at all," she protested weakly. "It was all set decoration, entirely for the multitude."

"Balls. Sorry, love, but you could see the heat rising. Everybody was absolutely entranced."

She had certainly *felt* the heat. Her whole body seemed to liquefy as his lips smothered hers, and then turn to scalding steam. She had never experienced such a transformation in her emotions in all her life before. She could barely remember now how they had got off the stage and back to their seats again. She could still hear the cheers, but why the crowd had got so excited by a kiss, she couldn't guess. Something to do with his magnetism, she supposed.

"It didn't make the morning editions, of course, but it'll be in the *Standard* and the *Mail* for sure," Jenny informed her gleefully. "I've already been called by both papers, for the background. They'll be calling you in a minute, I bet."

On cue, the phone gave the Call Waiting beep in Dana's ear. "Hell," she said mildly. "That's one of them now. What did they ask you?"

"Oh, the usual—how long you've been seeing each other. When you gave Mickey the push."

Dana rolled her eyes. "Oh, ouch!" This was a complication that hadn't occurred to her. "I suppose he'll be furious."

"It was open to him to get on his horse some time ago, as I recall," Jenny said pitilessly. "If it's now come to a point where he's made to look redundant, whose fault is that?"

Dana sighed. "I know, but what can a man do when he thinks persistence is a virtue?"

"Why didn't you just tell him about your rugged sheikh in the first place?" Jenny laughed. "I'm sure that would have scared him away."

"Jenny, I only met him last night. There was nothing to tell."

"I believe you, darling, but millions won't. If that's the truth, it's the most rampant case of passion at first sight since...since—Adam saw Eve, I suppose. That—"

"No, it wasn't." The Call Waiting signal was still

beeping. Most callers would have hung up by now. Definitely either a journalist or Mickey. "He was after something, for sure, but it wasn't me. Sheikh Ashraf was playing a deep game, as they say."

Jenny was surprised into silence. "Really?"

"Really. It may have looked good, but he made it very clear to me that—"

"Look good? That kiss steamed up every pair of glasses in the room. It looked as if it would melt marble!"

Dana couldn't help the little buzz that went through her bones, the smile that toyed with her lips. "I didn't say the man couldn't kiss."

Jenny whooped with delight. "I knew it! I knew—"

"Jenny."

"I knew you'd been keeping something from me! Tell me all about it! Ooooh, the way he said *fifteen thousand pounds* in that determined voice, as if daring anyone to overbid him!"

"Jenny, I came home in the limo alone. He told me he was leaving town today and that I should take a friend along for that evening at the Riverfront he paid for."

"Awwww!" Jenny cried. She was genuinely disappointed. Jenny was a rare person—she had no envy. She wanted what was best for her friends, never projecting her own needs onto the situation. "Aw, Dana, I thought you had it made! A gorgeous sheikh at your feet, who could ask for better than that?"

"Well, it ain't gonna happen," Dana said. "Look, darling, this phone is going crazy in my ear. I'll have to take the other call. Can we talk later?"

"Yes, I'm due on set in a few minutes anyway. I'll call you again when I get a break."

* * *

"It worked well, then," Ashraf Durran ibn Wafiq ibn Hafzuddin al Jawadi said, tossing the *Times* to one side and picking up the *Telegraph* as he reached lazily for his coffee cup.

"It worked like a dream," Gazi al Hamzeh concurred. The two men sat at opposite sides of a table in a private jet flying high above the English Channel. "We covered all the bases, something for every paper from the nationals right down to *News of the World.*"

He pointed to the *Telegraph*'s front-page photo of Ashraf in the red jacket. Underneath was the caption *Sheikh Ashraf Durran was one of the dignitaries attending the Bagestani Drought Relief charity function in London last night. A Cup Companion to Prince Omar of Central Barakat, the sheikh is of mixed Bagestani and Barakati descent.*

Underneath was the small headline of a separate story: *Bagestan Living In The Hopes Of Discovering The Al Jawadi Heir.* The story mentioned Bagestan's unhappy plight under the monstrous dictator, President Ghasib, and how desperate the Bagestanis were to restore the monarchy through a direct descendant of ex-Sultan Hafzuddin al Jawadi. The problem was that after taking power in a military coup in 1969, Ghasib had embarked on a program of assassination of the al Jawadis. The entire family had been forced to live in exile under false names for three decades, and no one could say for certain whether any were still alive.

However, rumour was very strong within the expatriate Bagestani communities around the world that the al Jawadi family had successfully protected themselves except for the assassination of Sultan Hafzuddin's second son, Prince Wafiq, in the late seventies. Most Bagestanis believed that Wafiq had left two sons, now about thirty years old, and that one of them had been named Crown Prince by the old sultan before his death several years ago.

This man, it was rumoured, was now poised to take power from Ghasib. But who was he, and when would he show himself?

"Neat juxtapositioning," Ashraf remarked.

"Yeah," Gazi said. "It's absolutely textbook stuff. You can't say it straight up, so you run two stories side by side, and hope your readers are smart enough to get the drift. They certainly will be here. Not a Bagestani in town who won't put two and two together this morning.

"The upmarket afternoon tabloids will all carry the story of the outrageous bidding you did for Dana Morningstar—that's their kind of stuff—and the others will feature the kiss. Which, I have to say, was a powerful ad lib. For a minute there, even I thought you were going to come right out and declare yourself."

Ash shook his head. "Your campaign is too well thought out for me to fool with. Let's keep them guessing."

"Dana Morningstar played up well. She's a stunningly beautiful woman up close, isn't she?"

Ash's eye was caught by something in the paper and he didn't answer.

"Does she know?" Gazi pressed.

Ash shrugged, still reading. "She told me she thinks it's a fairy tale, and all the al Jawadi are dead."

"That's a bit odd, given the circumstances, isn't it?"

"It's possible she really doesn't know. Or maybe—" Ash lifted his head and eyed the public relations advisor thoughtfully. "She's estranged from her father, apparently. I wonder what's behind that."

The two men looked at each other for a pregnant moment while the implications sank in. "Hell!" Gazi exploded. "How is it we never found that out? She wouldn't be actually in the Ghasib camp, would she?"

Ash laughed and shook his head. "Stop worrying, Gazi. It was pretty obvious, when I thought of it, that she said what she said largely to irritate me. I overheard her say something and challenged her on it, and she's obviously a woman of spirit."

"It never even occurred to me to question whether the daughter of Colonel Golbahn was loyal to the cause. I should have. It should have been the first thing I checked."

"Well, it doesn't matter now if she isn't. The speculation will blow over in a few days, won't it?"

Gazi was staring gloomily into his cup. He shook his head. "It depends, Ash, doesn't it?"

"On what?"

"On what she does now. If she wants to pretend you're involved with her, she could say damned near anything about you, and after that show last night, she'll be believed."

"Forget it. She's not the type."

Gazi looked at him levelly. "Sure of that? She could wreck your chances with the religious, Ash. And you need the mullahs."

"She's got a grudge against her father, maybe, but if Dana Morningstar's actively rooting for Ghasib I am no judge of character."

"You are sure it's character you're focussed on, and not sex?" Gazi challenged him.

"Who says a man can only focus on one thing at a time?"

"When one of the things is sex, everybody. Remember, God gave man a brain and a penis, but only enough blood to run one at a time."

Ash laughed. "Dana Morningstar is not a traitor to the cause."

"All right, I hear you." Gazi shrugged. "Let's see what she does next."

Five

"For God's sake!" Roxy cried, wriggling through the apartment door as soon as Dana cracked it open. "What is going *on?* I've been trying to phone you for three days!"

Dana shook her head at her younger sister, closed and locked the door. "So has everybody else in London."

"Who? Why? What do they want?"

Dana shrugged, turned and led the way to the sofa in front of an open glass-paned door. Outside was a small, sunny terrace overlooking nearby roofs. "Media people, mostly. They want to talk to me about a) my breakup with Mickey, and b) my hot affair with the handsome sheikh who might or might not be one of the al Jawadi grandsons. Not necessarily in that order." She waved Roxy into a chair as she spoke, went into the kitchen and returned with another cup.

Tossing aside the script she had been reading, she

sank into an armchair. She poured a cup of tea, passed it over, then sipped from her own cup and looked at Roxy over the rim. "And what do *you* want?"

Roxy had the grace to look a little embarrassed. It was true she didn't often visit just on the strength of sisterly love. Roxy spent money fast and furiously, and although usually their father covered her amazing deficits, there were times when she had a reason not to apply to him.

"Well, it's not money this time," she said mulishly. "Or at least, it is, but this isn't about borrowing anything."

"Good," Dana said clearly. "Because maybe you've noticed I'm unemployed as of last week."

"Yeah, I heard you're getting dropped from the show. That's too bad. What happened?"

"Partly the new producer thought I should be more grateful than I was when he told me he had plans for Reena to become a more important character. Partly just the demand for constant change."

Roxy stared at her, the second part of this speech lost on her. "Really? Oh, wouldn't Daddy hate that! He always said that was what would happen if you went into acting."

A cloud moved, and the afternoon sunlight suddenly poured into the room. Dana, wearing snug-fitting shorts and a three-quarter-sleeve top in soft jade brushed cotton, slung her long legs up over one arm of her chair and rested her back against the other.

"I know he did. So what?"

"Do you always say no to producers, Dana?"

Dana lifted eyebrows in the suddenly haughty expression that had always made her sister just a little afraid of her. "Yes, I always say no," she returned shortly. "Are you going to tell me what the problem is?"

The physical resemblance between the two sisters was not strong. Dana's build was long and slender, and her strong-boned face had a nobility that was quite unlike Roxy's prettily rounded, softly fleshed body and features. They had different mothers, and each took after her mother rather than their mutual father.

There was more than six years age difference between the two girls, too, so it was perhaps natural that soft, sweet Roxy should so often come to strong, proud Dana for help and advice.

"Daddy talks about you a lot," Roxy said suddenly, ignoring her cue. "He'd really love to see you."

Dana shrugged. "Six-thirty p.m. Monday to Thursday, and an omnibus edition on Sundays at three."

"Aren't you ever going to relent, Dana?"

"Roxy. You don't understand, you have never understood. You grew up with both your parents there and loving you. I was robbed of my mother's love for ten years and five months. You will never know what it means to a five-year-old to be told her mother doesn't love her or want her and to live with that for ten years before learning that it was a lie."

"I'm not saying what he did wasn't wrong. I'm only saying maybe—"

"I know what you're saying. You've said it before." Her face took on an untouchable look that always made her sister nervous. "Now, do you want to tell me your problem or not?"

It had been ten years since the day Dana had learned of her father's terrible, unspeakable betrayal of his wife and daughter. Ten years since a tall, beautiful woman with a tragically lined, oddly familiar face had come up to her table in the little bistro near the private girls' school she attended.

"Dana? Are you—Dana Golbahn?"

"That's right," Dana said with an enquiring smile. She wouldn't smile so freely again for a very long time.

"Dana, I'm—" The woman licked her lips and to Dana's amazement tears burst from her eyes. "I'm your mother. I've been looking for you every day for the past ten years."

He had kidnapped her. He had left his wife without a word and taken his daughter away without even a last goodbye kiss. He had lied to his daughter—"Mommy doesn't want you. Mommy's tired and wants to be by herself,"—but to her mother he had been even crueller than that. Not a word. Nothing. She had come back from shopping one calm Saturday afternoon to find that her husband, her daughter, and her life had disappeared.

"I was frantic. Out of my mind with worry. At first I thought you must have had an accident in the car—well, I went on wondering about that for years. Even after all the evidence was in that he had planned it all, had taken your passport…even after the divorce papers arrived, I still had nightmares about a car being found in a lake with you inside it."

"But *why?*" Dana cried. All the nights she had sobbed herself to sleep, wanting her mother, her beautiful mother, and the stories about Nanabush and the Bear, *Mishi-bizheu* the Lynx, and the Anishnabek people. To her it was utterly incomprehensible.

Her mother said, "Your father fell in love with me against his will. He wanted me to convert, but I wouldn't. But I agreed that our children should be brought up in his religion. I didn't realize then that he would consider my telling you Ojibwa stories and tales

a violation of my promise. To your father, to talk about
Bear and Fox was to set up partners with Allah, the
worst kind of *shirk*.''

And with those words a host of memories flooded
back. Dana suddenly remembered her father asking her
what grace she had said over her food. ''I was thanking
the salmon for giving up his life for mine,'' she had
explained gravely. He had yanked her from the table,
slapped her, sent her to bed. There were a dozen other
moments like that—moments when he had tried to wipe
all trace of her mother's influence from her life.

And he had almost succeeded.

Dana was sixteen when her mother finally found her,
and going through a fairly normal teenage rebellion. The
meeting with her mother pitchforked her into a complete
rejection of her father and all he stood for. She refused
to spend another holiday at his home, instead going back
to Canada at every break to make up for lost time with
her mother.

It was the beginning of a strong, rich relationship.
After her loss, Alice Golbahn had returned to the res-
ervation where she was born and begun to study with
the medicine man there. Now she was a healer herself,
and mother and daughter worked together to mend the
rift in their lives during long walks through the forest
while they gathered herbs for Alice's medicines, long
chats while they dried and stored them.

Her relationship with her father suffered as that with
her mother blossomed. Dana had listened to her father's
explanations just long enough to establish that what her
mother had told her was true. Then she had turned her
back on him and all he stood for.

* * *

Roxy sat up and set her cup on the coffee table. "If I'm going to tell you I need something stronger than tea," she begged.

Dana nodded and got up to pour her a drink, her bare feet padding over the beautiful, hand-knotted Bagestani rug. The rug was only one of many signs in the apartment that Dana no longer turned her back completely on her Bagestani blood, however rarely she spoke to her father these days. "You kept me all to yourself for ten years," she had pointed out ruthlessly when she was sixteen. "Now it's my mother's turn."

She poured a glass of Roxy's usual chilled Australian Shiraz and handed it to her before sinking down into her armchair again. Then she waited.

Roxanna took a couple of healthy slugs and, staring down into the glass, muttered, "Well, you have to know. I got into debt at the casino again."

"Oh, Roxy!"

"I know, I know!"

"But *why?*"

"Because it's fun!" her sister snapped defiantly. "And because they encourage me, and because everyone else is doing it!"

"Everyone else is rich enough to lose. You aren't."

Roxy's chin set mulishly. Criticism was counterproductive with her. Dana shook her head. "How much have you lost?"

She couldn't believe her ears when she first heard the amount. The jolt brought her legs swinging around and she sat upright. She made Roxy repeat it, then stared at her.

"I don't believe this! Are you crazy? No one could lose that much money in a single night!"

Roxy began to cry. "It's bad, isn't it?"

"*Bad?* It's out of this world! It's utterly unbelievable!"

"I know, I know! Don't shout at me, I don't know how it happened! They just kept giving me more chips and I kept signing...."

"The casino must be cheating you. They faked some of the receipts or something."

Roxanna hiccupped on a sob. "No. The—the champagne's free, but all the signatures were mine. Oh, God, Dana, what am I going to do? You've got to help me!"

Dana stared at her blankly. "Help you? How? I don't begin to have money like that! Even if I sold this flat and the car—Roxy, what on earth do you imagine I can do about an amount like that? I doubt if even Dad could cover it."

The mention of their father made Roxy sob even louder. "This will kill Daddy! He can't find out! It will kill him!"

"Yes, I think it might," Dana said, because what was the point of mincing words? It wasn't just that their father had a weak heart. It wasn't just that gambling was forbidden by their religion. Roxy was his darling. The thought that she had been gambling again, after all his strictures, and had lost so dreadfully, would break him.

"But I don't see what choice you have, Roxy. He's got to be told. What else is there? You've got to raise the money somehow, or they'll— Dad told you before how dangerous those casino people are. He told you what they'd do."

Roxy sobbed more loudly.

"It will break him financially," Dana added, half to herself. "It'll take everything he has. He'll end up living in a council flat, if they give him one, on the state pension."

It was cruel, but she wasn't going to pretend. Roxy had been warned. And pretence would get them nowhere. This spelled ruin for their father, and quite possibly for Dana as well. But she at least had a career to turn to. Her father was retirement age.

"There *is* something else I can do," Roxy muttered when the spasm of crying had passed.

Dana heaved a breath. "They'll let you work in one of their brothels until you pay it off, I suppose. That's what Dad said, isn't it?"

"No, it's not that. They—they want two C U."

"They want what? What's a C U?"

Roxy got some strength from somewhere and lifted her head to look straight at her sister. "They want *to see you*."

Dana went very still, staring at her sister, all puffy face and pleading eyes. "They want to see me?" she repeated slowly, weighting each word. A chill of prescient horror slithered down her spine.

Roxy sniffed, nodded, dropped her eyes again.

"What do you mean, they want to see me? What did they say?"

"'Bring Dana Morningstar to see us.'"

Her stomach heaved. "Why do they think you could arrange that?"

"They know we're sisters."

Dana's jaw set dangerously. "Who told them? You?"

Roxy sniffed and shook her head. "I don't know how they know. They just knew. They showed me your picture in the paper and said, *Bring your sister to see us immediately.*"

"Or what?"

"Or they'll tell...oh, Dana, please go and talk to them! They'll tell Daddy! And oh, Dana, I know it will kill him. It was bad enough you becoming an actress! If he knows I've been gambling again—oh, God! You don't love him, Dana, but I do! He's my father and he's never done anything bad to me and I love him and I don't want him to have another heart attack!''

Rage drove Dana to her feet. ''Why didn't you think of that when you were disobeying him? You say I don't love him—how can you pretend to love him when you do a thing like this? What did you think was going to happen? Did you imagine you'd win all the money back if you just went one more round? How many times did you think that before the truth finally sank in?''

Roxy started to sob again. ''Dana, I'm sorry! I'm sorry!''

''Dad warned you what those people were like! He told you they like to get upper class girls into prostitution that way! Why didn't you listen?''

''I don't know, Dana!''

''If they think *I* am going to prostitute for them, they can think again. And you, too! Why didn't you tell them I wasn't an option? Would you really be willing to have me do a thing like that in your place?''

Her sister's sobs increased to heartrending wails. ''No, no! I'm sure it's nothing like that! I'm sure of it!''

''How can you be sure? How can you begin to guess how minds like that work? For all you know I'll walk in the door and be chloroformed and—oh, God, Roxy, this is just too ugly! This is unbelievable!''

''You see, Miss Morningstar, it is very simple. Your friend, Sheikh Ashraf Durran, is an old, long-established customer of our casinos, here and elsewhere. And—''

''I don't think it's quite as simple as you imagine. I have told you, he is no friend of mine, and that is the truth. I met him once in my life and he kissed me because it was part of a charity function.'' Dana tossed aside the tabloid with the screaming headline and the photo of that kiss. ''It was an act.''

It looked like a very passionate clinch. Her arms were by her sides, one elbow half bent, in helpless protest or in the first beat of passion, or both. Her back was arched a little over his arms, one arm like a bar at her waist, the other on the bare skin of her upper back. Both their faces wore an expression of passionate abandon as her lips parted under his.

She remembered the kiss, the heat of his hand, the skill of his mouth, with a sudden, primitive immediacy that brought the blood to her cheeks. She had never in her life thought she was going to faint because of a kiss, but all the tension of the evening had seemed to surge back as she looked up at him, and his arms had been so passionately possessive she had stopped breathing on a gasp.

He had been talking about hunger, the hunger of the people, but her heart heard it as his, her, their mutual hunger. That strong mouth, those fierce eyes, and when his kiss smothered her she had felt devoured by his passion. Her mind knew it was fakery, but her body and soul had responded as if to a central truth.

Desire had erupted through her, a black, stunning jolt of electricity that blotted out all thought, leaving her at the mercy of pure sensation. Lightning had danced on her lips and skin, thunder rolled through blood and bones.

But she wasn't telling this man that. She fought down the heat in her blood and gazed at him in cool enquiry.

The man nodded. There was an inhuman aura which she found horrible, the stench of a rotting soul.

"You are an actress, Miss Morningstar, and I must allow you to be the expert on such matters as acting. But I am a man, and you in your turn must allow me to tell you that for the sheikh it was not an act. He was a man distracted by your beauty."

She couldn't quite place him or his accent. Wherever he had originated, and Bagestan was a possibility, he had clearly been living in the West for many years—but not in England. Australia or South Africa, she thought.

She shrugged, to hide the little whisper of echo in her that said it was true. He had not been unmoved by the kiss. "Much good may it do him, if you're right," she said.

The man nodded. "Let us not argue the matter. You are here because your sister foolishly gambled more than she had at the tables. If she does not pay her bill, I will approach your father and demand payment. It is of no moment to me, but I understand that your sister is reluctant for me to do this. You, too, or you would not have come."

Dana lifted a careless eyebrow. "It won't do you any good if you do—my father hasn't got money like that."

His gaze ran over her face with a knowing smile. "And of course your father has no friends to whom he could apply."

"Ask a friend to pay off his daughter's gambling debt? You don't know my father!" Dana said. He was making an insinuation that she didn't get, but she knew better than to let him see that it was so.

"Well, she preferred to go to you. Now, I'll be frank with you, Miss Morningstar. Large as it may seem to you and your sister, her debt is pocket change to us. We would be quite happy to write it off to experience—if we had a good reason to do so."

She flicked an eyebrow at him, but did not speak, and he went on, "There are other debts that aren't so small or so easy to write off. Sheikh Ashraf Durran ran up a debt here last winter that would make your hair stand on end. Millions of pounds. And then he ran out. He has not been in England long enough for us to get a bead on him since then. He has bodyguards, so none of our process servers has a chance in hell of getting close."

She was surprised, and a little disappointed, to find such a weakness in Sheikh Ashraf. But then her father had always been a morally upright man on the outside, too, and look what he had done. That was the worst of puritans, she thought. They lived a lie.

He lifted a finger and pointed at her. "That's where you come in."

Her eyebrows went up. It was all a game of bluff. "Really?" she said unconcernedly.

He leaned back in his chair, bent his arm and pointed at her again. "You could get close to him—no, don't tell me you don't know him, it may be the truth, I don't know and it's immaterial. The point is, you could get to know him. You could get under his skin."

"And then what?" Dana asked, with a coolness she was far from feeling. *You could get under his skin.*

"Then nothing. You just let us know where he's going to be one night, so we can serve a subpoena on him." He flattened his hands. "That's all. That's all there is to it. He's in the south of France at the moment.

"We'll set you up first class, Miss Morningstar, and send you out there, all expenses paid. We'll make sure you meet up with him again. All you have to do is let the attraction blossom."

Six

_____

It hadn't been the most pleasant way to discover how much she still loved her father, Dana reflected two days later, stepping out onto the balcony of the world-famous hotel overlooking Cap d'Antibes' beautiful bay.

She had sat there, willing herself to say no and dare them to do what they could. But she knew, better than they, that they could do terrible damage. Roxanna was her father's darling; he doted on her.

He was a proud man. Dana had always known that she inherited her stubborn pride from her father. He would do whatever was necessary to wipe away Roxy's debt, but living with the consequences would break him. To be dependent on government handouts after a life of hard work and tragedy overcome...

All these things about her father she knew and had always known. What had surprised her had been her own heart's response. She couldn't do it. She couldn't let it happen to him.

Her agent had not been happy about the prospective open-ended holiday, until she learned where Dana would be going. "You're bound to meet people, Dana!" she'd enthused then. "Especially at the Eden Roc! Do some networking!"

They had told her she would get the star treatment, and she had. She had travelled first class, been met by a limousine. Her suite was utterly luxurious, on the third floor of the legendary Eden Roc Hotel, home to the stars.

They had insisted on supplying her with a wardrobe, saying she had to look the part, had to be able to mix with the rich and famous here. And once she had agreed in principle to their main demand, it seemed futile to waste energy arguing over details. They were right—she was an actress and she had to be costumed for the part she was playing.

She had no intention of fulfilling the spirit of the demands the casino owners had made on her. She had come here to save her father. But she was not going to try to insinuate herself into Sheikh Ashraf Durran's life or his bed.

She had to make it look good. The casino owner had hinted that he would have spies around her, and she didn't doubt that. So she was going to try to meet the sheikh again, all right. But what she planned to say to him wasn't on the casino owner's agenda.

The motor launch bucked over the swell under the shimmering afternoon sky and pulled up beside the megayacht. *Dhikra,* read the name on the bow, in large, lazy script, and underneath it, the same word in the more graceful Arabic alphabet. *Dhikra. Remembrance.*

Gazi al Hamzeh leapt out onto the landing platform and ran lightly up the steps to the deck above. "Where is he?" he asked of the nearest deckhand, who pointed aft.

He found Ash, barefoot and bare chested, sitting at a table spread with papers and books—documents, legal submissions, texts, and a Qu'ran. He had a yellow legal pad beside him and was making notes. When Gazi opened the door, he tossed down his pen and stood. The two men embraced and kissed cheeks in the Eastern manner.

"How's it going?" Gazi demanded.

Ash shrugged and stretched out the kinks of hours of paperwork. "Everything's looking good, Gazi. If we can trust the commitments we're getting, we've got it almost sewn up. The parliamentarians we pinpointed all look promising. As for the *ulema*—"

He lifted strong tanned fingers to rub his eyes.

"Giving you troubles?"

"They're making a lot of demands. They have agreed in principle to a secular government, but now they want the constitutional code of human rights we're drafting watered down in certain areas."

"Alcohol and women's rights," Gazi guessed, flinging himself down into a chair.

Ash nodded. "And a couple more, but those are the main ones." He gestured at the table. "I've been reading through legal and religious opinions of the past couple of centuries."

"Well, we know you aren't going to win over the extreme leaders," Gazi said. "But you don't need me to tell you you've got to have some of the moderates on board."

Ash grimaced. "No, you don't have to tell me. It's a

question of the minimum necessary compromise, isn't it? But I don't like it. As far as alcohol goes, I've tried to explain that too much of the economy currently is tourism-based. I've told them what would happen to the industry if the hotels and restaurants were suddenly forced to go dry, but—''

He broke off and looked more closely at Gazi's face, realizing this was not what had brought him here. "What is it?"

"There's been an unpleasant development on another front," said Gazi, looking a bit *I-told-you-so*.

"What front?"

"The daughter of Colonel Golbahn arrived last night. Dana Morningstar. Checked in to the Eden Roc."

Ash took it in silence, his eyes going slightly distant as he absorbed the implications. After a moment he nodded. "Right," he said.

"Too much of a coincidence, Ash," Gazi said sadly.

"She's an actress, Gazi, and this is the summer playground of movie people."

"There's more to it. She'll—uh—Lana Holding had a call from a press agent in London. Fed her some story about building up Morningstar's presence in advance of a film being released next month. Lana says that came across as eyewash. She owes the agent a favour and she says she should do it. She wanted to know how we felt about it."

"Should do what?" said Ash.

"Treat Morningstar as an A-list celebrity, which of course she isn't, not here in film star land. And include her in tomorrow's fund-raiser."

Dana's heart was thumping as she slipped out of the limousine, stepped onto the red carpet and glanced up.

A large red-and-green banner over the massive bronze entry doors read *The Night of the Thousand and One Books: The Parvan War Relief Celebrity Storytelling Event*.

There were a few cheers and cries of "Reena" in English voices from the crowds behind the barriers on either side of the carpet as she mounted the broad steps to the entrance, and that was more than she had expected. Most of the crowd here wouldn't recognize her. An English soap star didn't rank very high in Cannes. But there was plenty of speculative whispering as she passed, probably because of her costume.

An official from the Parvan War Relief charity met her at the door as eagerly as if she were a hot Hollywood property. "Miss Morningstar! Dana!" she cried in a warm voice, and the crowd shifted and began to wonder if they should know her after all.

"I'm Lana Holding," the woman said, taking her arm and leading her into the brilliantly lighted hall, and Dana suddenly recognized her. Lana Holding al Khosravi was the charity organizer who was almost as well-known as the celebrities she regularly persuaded to take part in her imaginative fund-raising events. These were for the benefit of the tiny kingdom of Parvan, whose three-year war had so devastated the country. She was married to a Parvani herself, and was the daughter of Jonathan Holding, the American computer mogul. She used her own name professionally.

"You look terrific! Thank you so much for agreeing to take part in this," Lana enthused. The slender redhead escorted her down the length of the crowded foyer along a cordoned-off path, explaining the event as they walked.

"Of course no mingling with the audience before the

show,'' Lana explained when Dana asked. ''Everyone is in the Green Room tonight. But if you'd mingle a bit in here afterwards, we'd be very grateful. That's really what they pay for.''

A black-suited attendant opened a door with a flourish and Lana led her into the Green Room. All around the room famous people from different media and many countries, and in an interesting variety of costumes, were drinking, laughing and chatting.

Dana was wearing soft white deerskin, a long slender skirt with a fringed hem, a sleeveless top with an intricate beadwork design in turquoise and green, and matching dangly feather-and-bead earrings. A beadwork headband clasped her forehead and her hair streamed out over her shoulders. On her feet were matching beaded moccasins. It was an outfit one of her mother's friends had made for her. She looked like an Ojibwa princess.

Some of the celebrities had really taken the dictum ''dress relevant to your performance piece'' to heart; others had only given it the nod. One star dressed in tight shimmery black and outrageous feathers was fairly obviously going to be reading a story with a Wicked Queen in it, and an aging, rather alcoholic English stage actor was making a virtue of necessity: he'd be reading from *The Lost Weekend* or something similar, Dana guessed.

A Hollywood actor had come as Mark Twain, and an English actor, very predictably, was Shakespeare. A French actor she had always wanted to meet was, she guessed, meant to be the great fabulist La Fontaine.

Dana's heart gave an uncomfortable kick and there was Sheikh Ashraf Durran. It was the first time she had seen him since the night of the kiss; he had not been at this afternoon's brief rehearsal.

He was dressed like a fairy-tale caliph in a navy blue silk coat intricately embroidered in white, gold and red, a long gold-embroidered sash wrapped around his hips, flowing Middle Eastern trousers and curl-tip embroidered red leather slippers. A curved scimitar hung from his waist in an intricately decorated scabbard, and one dark hand rested negligently on the jewelled hilt. On his dark hair was a navy turban, tied with the ends falling over one shoulder.

Dana actually gasped as her eyes fell on him, as if some shock had been delivered deep to her system. He looked stunningly, exotically male. And powerful, Dana reflected, like a magician in a fairy tale. She slowed her steps as Lana Holding led her past him, and as if unconsciously drawn by her interest Sheikh Durran turned his head.

This might be a good time to talk to him, if only to say she had something to tell him and arrange to meet later.

She smiled, suddenly understanding how much she was looking forward to another meeting. She had not counted that as one of her reasons for giving in to the casino owner's demands, but perhaps, unconsciously, it had been.

"Hello again," she said, her voice warm.

His expression hardened as he recognized her. It showed no vestige of friendliness or even good humour. Dana caught her breath, wondering how she had offended him. His black gaze seemed to burn right through her.

"Oh, that's right, you two know each other!" Lana Holding exclaimed with a laugh.

"Ye—" Dana began, but Sheikh Ashraf's harsh voice overrode her.

"We have met. Hello." He nodded briefly at Dana and deliberately turned back to his companions.

Dana bit her lip and turned away, feeling humiliated and angry. He had treated her as if she were a starstruck fan who was always pestering him! Lana chatted brightly to cover the awkwardness and led her across the room to where several English actors were raucously laughing.

Dana knew most of them, one way or another, and she was welcomed into the group with loud bonhomie. It was balm to her hurt pride and, childishly, she hoped that Sheikh Durran noticed.

At eight o'clock they filed through a door onto the stage, where a large semicircle of sofas and armchairs around the perimeter defined the central space. Downstage centre were two large, comfortable armchairs, angled towards each other.

Lana Holding made a speech about the progress of the ongoing landmine clearance program in Parvan, to which the funds raised tonight would be devoted. Her speech was moving and short, proving her expertise at fund-raising, and she quickly passed the mike over to the night's MC.

"...We asked our celebrities to come with a favourite story or poem. They have chosen from all the spectrum of world literature. There will be stories you know by heart and stories you have never heard before, short stories and long stories, true stories and stories of wisdom, fairy tales and myths and legends. We ask you please not to applaud each individual story, but wait until the curtain falls at the interval and the end of the show before you show your appreciation. Now we're going to dim the lights...."

So it began. There were no introductions. Each storyteller simply got up and silently moved to sit in one of the chairs at centre stage as the person preceding them vacated it, just as they had rehearsed it. The soft light went alternately up and down on the two central chairs. The audience was obedient and there was no applause to slow the proceedings.

The timing was expert, the evening was beautifully organized, and soon the audience relaxed, trusting that they were in the hands of masters, and slipped into the childlike willingness to be entranced that was essential to a successful evening.

Some people simply read from books they had brought with them, a poem or a children's story or something taken from books like *Morte d'Arthur* or *The Canterbury Tales*. Some recited poetry by heart. When Dana's turn came, late in the first half of the program, she did not begin by opening a book and reading the title. Instead, as the lights came up on her, she began softly,

"Among the Anishnabek, my mother's people, storytelling is a very ancient tradition. But we do not read our stories from books. Each storyteller retells a story in their own words, so that a story is a little different every time it is told."

She paused. The silence in the hall was profound. "Tonight, I am going to tell you the story of Nanabush, Coyote Woman and the Duck Egg," she said.

She told the story simply, in her warm, deep voice, then got up and moved back to her seat, and the next story started. When the curtain came down at the interval the applause was warm and prolonged.

They all filed back into the Green Room, congratulating Lana Holding on a brilliant idea brilliantly organized. There was a photographer making the rounds asking people to go and pose where he had lighting set up in one corner.

When Dana entered the room, Sheikh Durran was almost directly opposite the doorway. He was talking to Lana Holding. Dana stood irresolute. She was torn between feeling she had to try again to talk to him, and a furious determination never to speak to him again.

She was angry with herself, too, for the naive arrogance of the plan she had half-formed. She had planned to tell Sheikh Ashraf the entire truth, and ask him to accept the subpoena.

In London, remembering the moment when he had kissed her, she had imagined that he might listen to her, might do what she asked. Well, she was miles from being able to do that, though she wouldn't understand the reasons for his attitude to her if she thought about it for a year.

But she couldn't just give up without making any effort at all. Khalid Abd al Darogh wouldn't accept failure from her easily.

She had to try. It infuriated her. She would rather be boiled in oil than try to speak to Sheikh Durran again. But she had to try, or let her father sink.

Dana was in a daze, and didn't realize it until the photographer's assistant came up and startled her with a request to pose. She turned to follow him to the corner where the photographer was snapping people in quick succession.

"I wonder if you'd mind—it'll make a great shot—" she heard, as the photographer guided her into position.

"What?" Dana asked, and turned to see Sheikh Durran coming towards her, shepherded by another of the photographer's assistants.

"Oh—but..." Dana began, in awkward refusal, not

wanting to be exposed to another public rebuff, but the sheikh was smiling and saying, "Of course."

She wondered if she was the only person who saw the glint of anger in his otherwise bland expression. He came and stood beside her, and she could feel his heat against her bare arm. She couldn't resist a glance towards his face. He was looking at her, and the contempt in his face burned her.

"This was not my doing!" she snapped before she could stop herself.

He only raised his eyebrows and turned his head obediently as the photographer cried, "This way, please!"

He was working fast, only a couple of clicks and whirrs and the assistant was thanking them and moving them out of the way for the next subject.

Dana suddenly realized it was now or never. She would not get near him again, his expression told her that. "I need to talk to you," she muttered. "There's something—"

To her fury, he smiled, bowed his head, and simply turned away without a word.

Seven

"**O**nce upon a time there was a king. His name was Malek.''

Sheikh Ashraf Durran was the last speaker of the night, and Dana could see why. His stage presence was completely compelling. From the moment he had moved to centre stage, even when his chair was in shadow and the occupant of the other chair was reading, she couldn't keep her eyes away from him.

He had announced no title, given no introduction. He was sitting in a wide, easy lotus position in the chair, his scimitar resting across his knees, one hand lightly clasping it. He looked like a miniature painting of a Bagestani storyteller, painted on two inches of ivory, which was one of her father's treasures.

"Malek was not a great ruler, nor as wise as he should have been, but he was a good and honourable king. He ruled his people mildly and with as much justice as was possible in a troubled world. Nor was his kingdom a powerful one—there were many richer and more powerful kings in the world.

"In fact, one of King Malek's chief problems was how to maintain his nation's independence against the competing interests of two very powerful rival kings who were constantly trying to destroy each other. These kings were always looking for allies. They kept bringing other kings under their sway, and sometimes would urge these minor kings in their camps to fight. This was a cloak and a way to fight each other in limited war, for they were so powerful that to fight open war against each other would have destroyed them both.

"King Malek had, however, one source of wealth which these other kings envied and coveted. It was a mine of liquid gold. The two rival kings wanted this gold very much. They each tried everything to make the king declare his allegiance to one or the other and give them the gold.

"But the good king would not do so. He extended the hand of friendship, but he would not bend the knee of obeisance. And so the hearts of the powerful kings grew hard against him, and each suspected him of secretly conspiring with the other. And although neither king could risk taking Malek's tiny kingdom by force, for fear of what the other would do, they each waited for an opportunity.

"Now, King Malek took as one of his exemplars the great Caliph Haroun al Rashid. Imitating him, the king used to go out among his people in disguise, to see for himself how the kingdom was faring and how his appointed officials and others performed their duties. So the officers of the law and the judges of his courts and the dispensers of his charity were always fearful lest the person whom they treated unjustly or demanded a bribe of might prove to be King Malek himself.

"One day, while the king was walking in disguise in a street of poor homes, he saw a group of children playing. They were playing soldiers. One of the boys so impressed the king with his leadership and his grasp of military strategy that the king called the child to him and asked his name. He learned that Baltebani was an orphan, living in poverty with his uncle, who had no money to educate him or give him a trade.

"And so the king adopted the boy. Not as his heir, for Malek had sons of his own, one of whom would succeed him. Instead he educated the boy for the army. As the years passed he was rewarded with the youth's dedication and triumphs, for Baltebani lived up to every early expectation. And a deep trust and love developed in the king towards his adopted child, as strong as if Baltebani were his own son.

"When the boy had grown to manhood, the king created a new post, appointing him leader of all his armed forces, the first person other than the king himself to have this combined role, and thus the highest honour of his profession.

"I mentioned that the king had sons. He had three. One of them, Walid, the son of the king's favourite wife, Banu, grew up wise and true, and worthy to rule, and on his twenty-first birthday the king declared feasting throughout the kingdom. He named Walid Crown Prince in front of the people, declaring him his heir, and gave into his keeping a rose. That rose was the symbol of the family, and by tradition it passed into the guardianship and the responsibility of each Crown Prince on the day that he was appointed.

"Baltebani looked on at this ceremony, and envy was

born in his heart. He knew that he was as capable as Crown Prince Walid, and he told himself that if he had been in truth the king's son, Malek would have chosen him rather than Walid to succeed him. He wondered in his heart why blood should dictate the king's choice. For it was no longer the fashion in the world for kings to pass power to their sons. Some took power by force, and some by the will of the people, but few by virtue of blood.

"And the Commander of All the King's Forces asked himself if he should not gain power by one of the other methods."

The audience drew in a soft communal breath that moved like a whisper of wind across a lake. The beginnings of understanding stirred in them. The sheikh's voice was deeply compelling, and his story had drawn them in so that the entire hall was wrapped in silent, shared intimacy.

"I told you that King Malek had powerful enemies in distant kingdoms, kings who pretended friendship for the sake of the liquid gold, but who were waiting for opportunity. They saw it in Baltebani. The king himself trusted his commander so far that he did not notice how carefully Baltebani was choosing the men he appointed to leadership within the forces. The man had, from the earliest opportunity, and with the king's good will, been bringing into the military members of his own family. His brothers and cousins and even the friends from childhood with whom he had played his battle games had entered the army at his urging, and been promoted by his orders.

"Now these men were being moved to the highest positions in the armed forces, a fact which the foreign kings noticed, but King Malek did not. One of the foreign kings began to meet secretly with Commander Baltebani, and to aid him with money and advice, on the understanding that if the commander succeeded in taking power he would give the king access to the liquid gold his soul craved.

"And the day came when Baltebani turned on his benefactor and drove him out of the kingdom and took the throne in his stead. Every unit of the armed forces followed the commander's orders, save one. The leader of the Palace Guard alone was a position still appointed by the king. Because this man remained loyal to his sovereign when the call came, the lives of the king and many members of his family were saved, and they escaped secretly to exile in neighbouring kingdoms.

"Crown Prince Walid was murdered, but his infant son survived, hidden in the palace. The Crown Princess disguised herself as a serving woman, and for a week she washed the laundry of the new ruler in the palace, before the leader of the Palace Guard helped her to escape, carrying her baby son in a load of laundry. He personally led her to safety in a neighbouring kingdom.

"What had happened was not approved by the people, who wanted their king back. King Malek appealed to his powerful friends, those distant kings, for support in regaining his throne, and it was then that he understood how deeply he had been betrayed.

"He knew he could not regain his throne when Baltebani had such a powerful ally to support him. All he could do was start a destructive war against Baltebani—like so many kings before him, he would be funded by one powerful rival king, and Baltebani by the other. The country would be destroyed. And this he could not bring himself to do.

"So Baltebani was king, as he had dreamed. But his

conscience did not allow him to sit easy on his stolen throne. Perhaps because he understood betrayal so intimately, he feared there would be an attempt to restore King Malek or one of his sons to the throne, and so he sent assassins out into the world to seek out and kill King Malek's family.

"One of Malek's surviving sons was brutally slain in a distant country, and then King Malek understood his protégé at last, saw what an evil heart beat in the one he had promoted to such power. He understood that Baltebani would never feel secure until all members of the royal family were dead.

"Then Malek ordered the family into hiding. They must live apart, and take different names to prevent the assassins finding them.

"But there was always someone to recognize a prince. After eight years, Malek's last surviving son was slain, almost breaking the old king's heart."

When the realization flowered fully in her, Dana saw that it had been growing for some time, the understanding that the story the sheikh was telling was true. It was the recent history of Bagestan, told in fairy-tale style. But she was still under the spell of his voice, and she didn't take in what that meant.

"By this time, the people in the kingdom were desperately unhappy. Baltebani had quickly grown into a monster. It was not only the royal family against whom he sent his assassins, but every citizen who expressed disagreement with his policies and methods. Those who spoke or wrote against his evil practices were thrown into prison, tortured, murdered, their families made destitute.

"Meanwhile, Amir, the son of Crown Prince Walid, lived and grew to manhood under a false name in a neighbouring country. And when he reached the age of twenty-one, Amir in his turn was named Crown Prince and given the rose by the ageing Malek, who never lost his belief that the faithless Baltebani would one day be overthrown by the will of the people, and the throne of his ancestors restored to the family.

"Then a separate tragedy befell Malek. The country to which Amir and his mother had fled, and whose king, knowing their secret history, had treated them well, was attacked and invaded by an enemy. Crown Prince Amir went to battle, and was killed.

"The rose was lost from the day Amir died. No one knew where he had kept it.

"This blow was the last. As they brought the body of his favourite grandson across the threshold, the old king was struck down and had to be carried to his bed. He remained there for the remainder of his days, which were short, never regaining his health.

"Malek had three other grandsons, and as he lay on his deathbed, he summoned them. With his last energy, the old king charged these men with the duty of continuing the struggle to regain the ancient throne of their forefathers, to unseat the hated and vicious Baltebani and free their people from terrible oppression.

"Malek named one of these three grandsons Crown Prince, and though he could not give him the rose, he charged him to find it if possible, and keep it to show to the people as a sign of legitimacy on the day he ascended the throne.

"The princes vowed, to the king and to each other, to do as their grandfather wished. They would work together to restore the throne of their forefathers. They knew that the rose was a powerful symbol of unity and hope for the people of the little kingdom. And so the first task they set themselves was—to find the rose.

"When they had the rose, they would declare themselves to the world, and with the people's help, drive the monster Baltebani from power.

"Of course Baltebani discovered their aspirations. He learned that they were seeking the lost rose, and he was determined to find the rose himself, and show it to the people as false evidence that he was the old king's chosen one.

"Another man, too, was seeking the rose, for his own purposes. And he was closest to it.

"But fate was on the side of the princes. The rose was hidden among other roses, and the agent of this third man was guided to the wrong flower. He plucked it and fled, with the agents of Baltebani in pursuit. And so the princes were left to pick the true rose in peace."

The auditorium was still mostly silent, but excitement was building in wild waves that flooded every heart and must soon erupt. Dana could feel it beating against her like a sea. Her own heart was thumping so hard she could hardly breathe.

God, was it him? Was he the one? A murmur broke out and was instantly shushed, because the sheikh was still speaking.

"And so the princes have the rose, the ancient sign of kingship of their family. Although they have been forced to live in other countries since the moment of their births, their love of their own nation is powerful in their hearts. They suffer with the sufferings of their grandfather's people.

"And with the help of the people, they are going to unseat the monster Baltebani and take back the throne of power, and restore peace and good government and above all *justice* to the kingdom at last."

Eight

"**D**ana, you have to *do* something!"

Dana sighed her exasperation into the phone. "Roxy, will you please listen to me? Things have changed. He's not just Sheikh Ashraf Durran, Cup Companion to Prince Omar, which was bad enough to begin with! He's one of the grandsons of ex-Sultan Hafzuddin, for all I know the Crown Prince-designate himself, and he as good as said they're involved right now in a campaign to unseat Ghasib!"

"I know, I know! It was all on the news." Roxy was momentarily diverted from her own concerns. "They said the audience rioted. Is that true?"

Dana smiled reflectively. Never had she seen an audience erupt with such excitement. She supposed she never would again. It was a once-in-a-lifetime thing. They exploded to their feet when the lights went down, cheering, howling, waving their arms. The wash of excitement that poured over the actors as they stood at the front of the stage taking their bows was as intoxicating as wine. She had never been so thrilled and moved to be a part of something.

"I guess you could call it a riot, yeah."

"Oh! Was it scary? Were you frightened?"

"No. It was the most thrilling moment of my career. If I never stand in front of another audience—well, I've had the ultimate moment. Nothing could ever match it."

"You always were the lucky one," Roxy said.

Envy was loud in her sister's tone, and Dana had always hated that.

"Look, what do you expect me to do now? They'll have guards all over him. I won't get within a mile of him."

"Dana you can't take these people's money and then do nothing in return! It's not right, and—"

This was going a bit far, even for her sister. Dana set her teeth. "Do not preach morals to me, Roxy. When it comes to taking money you have no right to, you have already won first prize, remember? That's why we're in this mess right now."

"Sorry!" Roxy said mulishly.

"I was willing to try, Roxy, but you have to see that this changes everything. Every journalist in the world will be trying to get an interview with him. Not to speak of all the expat Bagestanis desperate for a look at the man who may be their new sultan."

She suddenly remembered the way he had kissed her in London, and what he had said then. *You know who I am. I am going to do what you want me to do. The hungry, desperate people of Bagestan...* No wonder all the expats had been foaming at the mouth that night.

Half of them must have got it then. She couldn't believe she had been so slow herself.

"But you're so smart. You'll find a way."

"Roxy, has it occurred to you that I might get shot by his security guards?"

"That's ridiculous!"

"Is it? There are Ghasib's assassins to think of, and I am sure Sheikh Durran is thinking of them. They killed his father and two of his uncles, don't forget. He must be very twitchy right now. Come on! Even those madmen at the casino can't expect me to carry on after this."

But Roxy just didn't hear information that interfered with her wishes.

"But they *do!* They called me to ask how you were doing right after it was all on the news. They say they're going to tell Daddy the day after tomorrow. We've only got forty-eight hours, Dana. You've got to think of something!"

"Things are hotting up," Gazi said casually, flinging himself down onto his chair again. "That was Lana on the phone."

Ash, Harry and Najib looked at him. They were on board *Dhikra,* sitting on an aft deck in the bright Mediterranean sunshine. All around them was blue sea. No one had so far discovered that *Dhikra* belonged to him, though no doubt some enterprising journalist would find out soon enough.

"Apparently she's had a visit from a concerned Dana Morningstar. She has a message for you and has to deliver it to you personally."

Harry looked from Gazi to Ash and laughed. "I'll just bet she does! And the message is, *Here's some strychnine, love Ghasib.* Tell her no thanks."

But Ash shook his head. "No," he said. "I should have spoken to her before. We need to know what she wants. If she is from Ghasib and I send her away he may put in someone less obvious. If she's not from Ghasib, we need to know that, too."

Najib pulled his ear. "Could be risky, Ash. We don't know how he might be planning to use her."

"Warn her she'll be searched. Unless she swallows a bomb we'll be safe enough. But to be on the safe side, Naj and Harry better not be aboard. Nor you either, Gazi. I'll see her alone."

The helicopter touched down expertly on the yacht's upper deck, just behind a beautiful blue swimming pool, and waited only till Dana had clambered out and run clear before lifting off again. She stood for a moment gazing skyward at it, but when it moved into the sun she dropped her eyes and turned away.

Almost into Sheikh Ashraf Durran's arms.

"Good afternoon."

Dana's breath caught on a gasp of surprise and she put a hand to her chest in an unconscious bid to quiet her heart.

She was wearing white again—loose tie-waist cotton trousers and a man's shirt open over a tank top. Her slip-on espadrilles were white canvas. She had a drawstring bag slung over one shoulder, and white sunglasses held back her hair. The only colour in her outfit was a necklace of flat square wooden beads painted in bright colours against the warm skin of her throat, and matching square red earrings. Her lips were the same rich red.

She looked rich, expensive and successful, he thought. And very, very sexy.

"Good afternoon," she replied, a beat behind time as

she returned his gaze. He was looking very cool and masculine in a white kaftan with rolled sleeves and open at the neck. Her mouth stretched into a smile, which he sombrely did not return.

"This way," said Ashraf and turned to shepherd her down to a lower deck. At his bidding, she went down the stairs, through the luxurious yacht till they came to a stretch of open deck half shaded with an awning, where a manservant was waiting. Dana chose a seat in the shade and looked out over the glittering blue Mediterranean. In the distance, closer to shore, she could see other yachts, but save for one small launch there was nothing nearer than a few miles. They were heading out to sea. Ahead of them the water was empty.

A soft breeze blew. If paradise could be partly man-made, this was paradise.

"What will you have to drink?" Sheikh Ashraf asked politely. Suddenly she remembered the humiliation of their last meeting, and her heart hardened. More to spark a reaction than because she really wanted it, she asked for white wine and sparkling mineral water. The servant bowed and withdrew.

"You carry alcohol aboard?" she couldn't resist asking the sheikh.

He raised his eyebrows at her as he took the chair at an angle to hers. The day was hot, but Dana loved the sun. The breeze coming off the water was delicious, and in the shade she was perfectly comfortable.

"Why not?" he asked.

She shrugged. "But you don't drink yourself, do you?"

"I don't. Nor do I impose my views on my guests."

The servant returned with a tray and set it down on the table beside them. Sheikh Ashraf signalled him and he bowed and disappeared again. The sheikh picked up her spritzer and handed it to Dana. She took it with a murmur of thanks.

"Why don't you drink? Is it for religious reasons?"

"Alcohol dehydrates the brain. In hot countries its effect is intensified," he said, and Dana set the wineglass down beside her and wondered if she wouldn't be smarter keeping her wits about her today. "I don't drink because I don't feel the need for alcohol."

She discovered that she was fascinated by him. She really wanted to know what made him tick.

"Did you ever drink?" she pressed.

He sighed as if he found her questions tiresome but couldn't be bothered refusing to answer. "Yes, at two periods in my life I drank. The first was in my rebellious university days when, in common with many of my contemporaries, I believed in breaking every rule. The second was during the war when intervals of oblivion were necessary to maintain sanity."

The breath hissed between her teeth. The Parvan-Kaljuk War had been notorious for the atrocities committed by the Kaljuks against Parvan women and children.

"I'm sorry," she murmured.

Sheikh Ashraf poured himself a glass of mineral water.

"Tell me why you are here, Miss Morningstar." His voice was firm; he was a man used to command. Dana heaved a breath and took a sip of her drink.

"It's complicated. I don't really know where to begin."

He drank and sat holding his glass a moment between his knees, gazing down at it. Then he set it on the table and looked at her again. He didn't offer her any advice on where to start, she noticed. Many people would have said *begin at the beginning* or something like that. He merely looked patient.

She found herself alternately excited by his presence and irritated by his attitude. Trying to quell both responses, Dana took a deep breath and sighed it out.

"My sister," she began. Then paused and licked her lips. She didn't like having to expose Roxanna like this, but where was her story without that? He had to know. She looked up to find his dark gaze on her, an expression in his eyes she couldn't read. Her heart thumped.

How she wished she could have met him under better circumstances. She cursed herself for that stupid explosion at the charity ball in London—no wonder he didn't like her! All she had said about what fools people were to believe the al Jawadi would restore their throne, about how they were being taken in...! Bad enough in any case, but said to a man who was almost certainly one of the al Jawadi heirs... She wondered if he had thought she knew who he was when she spoke.

What a fool she was. What a man he was, but she would never get any closer to him than she was right now.

"My sister gambled away a fortune she didn't have at a London casino," she blurted out all at once. "The owner is now threatening to go to—to my father, and demand the money. It's so much money! My father could maybe pay it if—" she heaved a breath and gazed down into her drink "—if he sold absolutely everything he's got. But it's worse than that. Roxy—Roxanna had promised him she wouldn't do it again. He bailed her out last time, and he absolutely hated knowing that she had gambled. It's unIslamic and all that."

"How much is her debt?"

She told him, and he nodded, accepting it without a blink. "Fine," he said. His hand went out to an intercom beside his chair. He spoke into it in rapid Arabic that she didn't catch. It was a long time since she had spoken her father's language, and she suddenly regretted letting it get rusty.

"They called her in to talk to them—" Dana returned to her recital "—and my sister—"

She broke off as the manservant appeared with a small tray and set it down on the table in front of Sheikh Ashraf. On the tray were a pen and what looked like a chequebook. He picked up the fountain pen and unscrewed the lid.

"You need explain no further, Miss Morningstar," he said. "I will take care of it."

And under her astonished gaze, he filled out the cheque for the amount she had named. Dana stared at him in astonishment.

"What are you doing?" she choked.

"Shall I make it out to you, so that you can supervise your sister's repayment?"

She felt as though she had stepped into another dimension.

"What—what do you mean? Why are you...why should you pay for...?"

She ran out of steam and sat staring at him openmouthed.

Sheikh Ashraf looked at her. He ripped out the cheque and offered it to her. "Is not this why you came to me?"

"No! Why would I? Why would I even dream that you would pay—what do you...do you think I have some hold over you or something?" she babbled, horrified. "This isn't blackmail! I don't know anything about you!"

At this he tucked the cheque under the chequebook, screwed the cap back on his pen, and leaned back in his chair, watching her. "You can think of no reason why I would be willing to pay your sister's debt and relieve your father of such grief?"

Dana was quite certain that he thought the debt was her own. But that was beside the point. "None whatsoever," she said.

He took that with a thoughtful nod. "Then why have you come to me?"

"I was blackmailed into it," she said baldly.

Sheikh Ashraf didn't move, but she felt that his whole being was electrified by her words. "You were blackmailed," he repeated softly.

"The casino owner called my sister in to talk. He showed her a—" Dana dropped her head and spoke to her drink "—a newspaper with a photo of you and me at that charity thing. He…had jumped to conclusions, and he told Roxy to bring me to see him. I had no choice, I had to go."

"Yes, I see." His voice was so quiet and calm, and she realized suddenly that he would be the one you ran to in a crisis. Every time.

"They wouldn't believe there was nothing between us. They said, even if that was true, that I could—could start something if I wanted. They told me that you…"

"That I—?" he prompted, when she faded out.

"That you owe them a huge amount of money, ten times more than Roxy lost, and that you keep dodging when they try to serve you with a subpoena. They wanted me to come down here and get to know you, and then trick you into being someplace where they could come and serve you with whatever paper it is."

He laughed briefly. "Where were you to take me to receive these papers?"

"They didn't say anything about that. I got the idea that once I'd—established contact with you, they would let me know."

"What is the name of the casino?"

"Park Place," Dana told him, wondering how many casinos he owed money to.

"And what was in your mind when you did their bidding?"

"I had to pretend to agree. They threatened to go to my father and insist on being paid and…but I thought, if I could just tell you about it, maybe you could pay them what you owe them, or…or at least accept the subpoena…."

He was shaking his head long before she finished, and her heart sank.

"Miss Morningstar—Dana. I do not owe these men money. I do not gamble, at the Park Place casino or at any other. This was a story told you by men who have very different motives than the ones they pretended to reveal to you."

He spoke with complete conviction, and she believed him. She stared at him, licking dry lips. A whisper of danger seemed to hover in the air. "What motives?"

"Tell me the names of the men who spoke to you."

"Khalid Abd al Darogh and Fuad al Kadthib."

A shadow crossed his face, but he only nodded.

"What do they want?" she repeated, her voice croaking with dread.

He hesitated, then shook his head slightly, and she knew by the look on his face that he would not tell her anything more.

"The question is, what is now to be done?"

He reached for the mobile phone lying beside the intercom, picked it up and punched a couple of buttons. Then he stood up and moved out into the sun towards the stern. He lifted a hand as if in greeting.

"Harry," she heard him say, but then he bent his head and she could make out nothing more. As she watched him, she became aware that the yacht's engines had died, and the launch that had been trailing at a distance was now approaching them at speed. So they had been under surveillance all the time.

When Sheikh Ashraf closed the phone Dana got up to stand at the railing and watch two crew members drop the landing ladder. The other boat pulled alongside below and two men got out, moved quickly up the ladder and came aboard. They ran lightly to the aft deck.

"Ash!" one of them cried, with a certain degree of relief, giving his back a thump. He was as handsome as it got, and Dana smiled involuntarily. But she knew which face she preferred.

"This is Dana Morningstar," Sheikh Ashraf said. "Harry and Naj, Dana."

She had the funny feeling that she had met Naj before, but he didn't make any comment, and so she didn't mention it. But his face certainly looked familiar.

So did hers, apparently. "Hey, I've seen you on *Brick Lane!*" Harry told her with a grin. "It's a great show. That Reena, she's one *mean* woman!"

Dana smiled. "Well, she gets her comeuppance in a month or so, so stay tuned."

"She does? What happens?"

"I'm contractually bound not to tell you."

He lifted his hands to the bounding main. "Hey, we're in the middle of nowhere!"

She laughed and shook her head. "Sorry. We were

particularly warned about directional mikes being aimed at yachts in the middle of nowhere.''

''Dana has other interesting things to tell you about, however,'' Ashraf said, and they all sat down. Dana repeated her story for Harry and Naj.

The yacht rode gently on the swell as she spoke, the sun sparked from the creamy paint and the blue water, and the cooling breeze stirred her hair. The three men sat listening intently, and Dana had the sudden feeling of being in a dream. She couldn't quite understand how she had got here.

When she had finished her recital of the facts and answered a few questions, they all sat in silence, considering.

It was Harry who spoke first. ''Well, it would be easy enough to pay the debt and let Dana go back home.''

Dana longed to ask why that solution had occurred to him, but it didn't seem the moment. Ash merely gestured to the tray that was still resting on the table, with the cheque tucked under one corner.

''Yes.''

''But there's a more serious problem here. They probably won't stop trying to, ah…serve a subpoena on you just because they've lost Dana.''

The tone of his voice put the phrase ''serve a subpoena'' in quotes, and Dana mulled that over. The three men seemed to know something about Abd al Darogh and al Kadthib that she didn't, something so obvious it didn't have to be mentioned.

''Might be a good idea,'' Harry went on, ''to let them think this plan is working. They may not bother trying to come up with another.''

Naj nodded. ''It's the obvious solution.''

Then they all three turned and looked at her.

The Silhouette Reader Service™ — Here's how it works:

Accepting your 2 free books and gift places you under no obligation to buy anything. You may keep the books and gift and return the shipping statement marked "cancel." If you do not cancel, about a month later we'll send you 6 additional novels and bill you just $3.34 each in the U.S., or $3.74 each in Canada, plus 25¢ shipping & handling per book and applicable taxes if any.* That's the complete price and — compared to cover prices of $3.99 each in the U.S. and $4.50 each in Canada — it's quite a bargain! You may cancel at any time, but if you choose to continue, every month we'll send you 6 more books, which you may either purchase at the discount price or return to us and cancel your subscription.

*Terms and prices subject to change without notice. Sales tax applicable in N.Y. Canadian residents will be charged applicable provincial taxes and GST.

If offer card is missing write to: Silhouette Reader Service, 3010 Walden Ave., P.O. Box 1867, Buffalo NY 14240-1867

NO POSTAGE
NECESSARY
IF MAILED
IN THE
UNITED STATES

BUSINESS REPLY MAIL

FIRST-CLASS MAIL   PERMIT NO. 717-003   BUFFALO, NY

POSTAGE WILL BE PAID BY ADDRESSEE

SILHOUETTE READER SERVICE
3010 WALDEN AVE
PO BOX 1867
BUFFALO NY 14240-9952

''Dana's exactly where she would be if she had done exactly what she was told, and been successful,'' Harry mused, and she could see that he was only voicing the thought that was in all their heads.

A nervous chill ran over her skin, ridiculous on so hot a day.

''What does that mean?'' she asked.

''If the men who are blackmailing you believe that you've successfully seduced Ash, there are—'' Naj began.

Dana jumped. ''And how would I convince them of that?'' she demanded nervously.

Naj lifted a hand. ''There's no problem there, but let's leave that for a moment. There are two possible benefits,'' he continued, turning to the others. ''First, we draw their fire. We discover what it is they're really after. Second, they won't be looking for another way of doing what Dana's already doing, so we'll have one less thing to worry about.''

Harry and Ashraf agreed. She looked back and forth between them. ''I thought you knew what they were really after.''

''We have some informed guesses,'' Ashraf said. ''The guesses boil down to variations on a couple of possibilities. One is—''

''Yes?'' she prompted. She was feeling increasingly uncomfortable, without knowing why.

''That they are hoping to create some sort of scandal. If you establish a connection with me, it could be exploited in a dozen different ways. I am sure you can see that.''

''Through my confessions in the tabloid press, I suppose,'' Dana offered dryly.

''Possibly. There are also the law courts. You might

accuse me of assault or rape, for example. That would certainly engage our energies at what is a critical time.''

''You're assuming they have reason to believe I'd go along with something like that.''

''They may consider that they have enough leverage on you to force your cooperation,'' he pointed out gently.

Dana had to accept the truth of this. She was sure in her own heart that she would never have agreed to take part in blackening anyone's character with a false accusation or exposé, but the men she had dealt with couldn't be expected to know that she would balk at such a thing. They had forced her to do their bidding once, why not twice?

''What's the other possibility?'' she asked.

The three men shifted and exchanged glances, and again she felt that whisper of dread touch her.

It was Ash who spoke. ''They may want to kill me. Your role may have been—to set me up for assassination.''

Nine

"**N**o!" she cried, as the whisper of dread became a dank, heavy cloud and settled over her, reaching sickening, cold tendrils into the marrow of her bones. She had never felt such horror. It wasn't like the movies at all. It was dreadful. She had sat with those men, talked to them...and they had been forcing her to unknowingly conspire in—

"No! Assass—*murder?*"

"It is one very strong possibility."

She saw it all, as if it were playing out before her eyes. She would have told them that the sheikh was going to be at a certain place, at a certain time...it was not a subpoena, but death that they would have delivered.

"Oh, God!" Dana cried, her hands at her mouth, her eyes black and staring at Sheikh Ashraf. Chills were coursing up and down her back, her arms, from her toes to her scalp. "What if I hadn't told you? What if I'd just...done what they said?"

"*Alhamdolillah,* you did not choose that path."

"Who are those men?" she demanded, half seeing the answer as she spoke. "Who are they?"

Again, that exchange of glances among the three. It was Naj who spoke. "They are men who have a very good reason to want to keep Ghasib in power in Bagestan."

Dana shuddered. She felt dirty, covered in filth. "Do you mean I've been working for agents of Ghasib? For—for Ghasib himself?"

"Khalid Abd al Darogh and Fuad al Kadthib own sixty-five percent of all the casinos in Bagestan," Harry said. "They naturally want to keep him in power, but whether they are actively conspiring with him or not—" He shrugged. "We don't know."

"But I don't understand," Dana said, turning to Sheikh Ashraf. "My sister went to that casino before I ever met you at the charity thing. Why would they—"

"Some of it was probably a lucky chance for them," Ash said. "The Park Place casino is known for trapping young women of good family into heavy gambling losses. Then they offer to let them pay the debt through high-class prostitution. They fly them to wealthy clients in Bagestan and elsewhere. Either your sister fell by chance into that trap, or one of the women already trapped was instructed to entice her into it."

She stared at him. "Instructed to entice Roxy in particular? Why?"

"They might have felt that to have Colonel Golbahn's daughter in such a position would be useful to them."

Dana didn't see that. She shook her head uncomprehendingly. "And then I met you by chance and they changed tactics to suit?"

He lifted his well-shaped hands as if it were self-evident.

She had the feeling that the pieces didn't quite fit. But there was too much to take in for her to assess it all. She suddenly realized that she had been sitting forward in her seat, tense and anxious, for a long time. She leaned back in her chair, letting herself feel the heat and the breeze, her fabulous surroundings. The sun was low in the western sky, and it would be setting soon.

It was so beautiful. After a moment she took a deep, relaxed breath and picked up her drink, which the servant had refreshed without her noticing. She looked from one to the other of the men as they spoke. In the strong, slanting light of the sun now coming in under the awning, a subtle physical resemblance between them became visible.

Harry looked at his watch. "I've got to get back to *Ma Fouze* before dark."

"Right," Naj said, getting to his feet. He lifted a hand. "Nice meeting you, Dana."

Dana set her drink down and stood up to say goodbye. As the two men left she moved over to the railing and watched them go down. Sheikh Ashraf went with them to the main deck, then watched as they moved down to the landing platform.

When the launch had left, cutting a wide arc away from the yacht, and the deckhand was drawing the ladder up against the side of the yacht, Sheikh Ashraf started back up the stairs to where she was waiting at the top. He looked up as he came, and their eyes met, and Dana's heart contracted with sudden feeling. *I want to be the one who waits for you,* she thought.

As he stepped up the last step and came towards her his presence was overpowering. There was a kind of electricity surrounding him; she could feel it envelop her.

She tried to smile it away, but couldn't. "I suppose you'd better call the helicopter now."

Sheikh Ashraf frowned in surprise, putting a hand out to her elbow, then withdrawing it. "Helicopter?"

Her pulse kicked. "I should get back to the Eden Roc. Unless there's something else to discuss?"

His face was suddenly without expression. "There is nothing to discuss if you have already made your decision."

"What decision?" she said stupidly.

"Have you decided not to stay?" the sheikh pressed, with some impatience.

Her heart seemed to leap into her mouth. She had never felt so stupid. "Stay where?"

"But what is solved if you leave now?" he demanded impatiently, as if he had expected her to understand something. "Where will you go? Back to London? What will you tell the men who sent you?"

He was right. She had been so geared up to the task of meeting him and telling him her story that she hadn't thought beyond it. She had hoped that talking to him would solve Roxy's problems. But nothing was solved—unless she took that cheque he had offered her. And she couldn't do that. She was back at square one.

"I don't know." She licked her lips. "Uh—I'll have to think. I didn't actually think about it—I couldn't plan when I had no idea what you would say."

She felt at a huge disadvantage with him. He was powerfully masculine and attractive, and being near him didn't do her reasoning brain any favours. He was looking at her with a dark look that she found deeply sexy, though she was certain he didn't mean it that way.

"You still haven't heard what I am going to say."

"Haven't I?" She blinked. She turned her head in confusion and her eyes happened to fall on the cheque he had written, still lying tucked under his chequebook on the tray.

"I see," the sheikh said in a changed voice. "Yes, of course. In that case, there is nothing more to say."

He bent down, picked up the cheque, and straightened to hand it to her. "Thank you for coming to warn me. I will call for the helicopter. Can I offer you another drink while you are waiting?"

Fury overcame her. How dare he make such an assumption about her? She snatched the cheque from him and tore it three times in quick succession and, staring into his face, tossed the eight little ragged bits of paper down. They were instantly snatched by the breeze and scattered across the pristine teak deck.

"There is no need to speak to me in that tone of voice," she snapped furiously. "I have no intention of taking money from you, Sheikh Ashraf, now or ever! But I really don't see what else there is to talk about! What do you want from me?"

He laughed, and again she was struck by how laughter changed him. A treacherous little thought flickered across her mind—*you have too many cares. If I were your lover you would laugh more.* She shook her head impatiently.

"Of course there is something to talk about," he told her, his white teeth flashing against his warm skin. "Did you not understand the point Harry was making when he said you were in the very position you would have been in had you obeyed al Kadthib?"

"No." She had been too busy looking at them, perhaps, and hadn't concentrated on what they were saying.

"I have ordered dinner. Will you stay to dinner with me, Dana, and hear what I ask of you?"

Her heart pounding with a mixture of fear and anticipation, she agreed.

She was shown into a stateroom by Sheikh Ashraf, who opened the door on a closet that was hung with women's clothes.

"These belong to my brother's fiancée," he said. "She is much shorter than you, but she would be happy for you to make use of whatever you can. Most of these things are new."

"Where is she now?" Dana asked.

"On board the *Ma Fouze* with Harry. It is a sailing yacht, so doesn't have much closet space. In any case, Mariel says she doesn't need such clothes when they are sailing."

She was too aware of his presence in the bedroom, too conscious of the large bed. She was glad when he showed her quickly around and left.

In the bath the taps and fittings were gold, and Dana couldn't help laughing. She took a cooling shower, but ignored the closetful of clothes to dress again in her own. She wasn't sure what was going to be suggested tonight, but she didn't want to look as though she thought she was moving in.

When she emerged, night had fallen. Music was playing softly, a Middle Eastern instrumental number. A servant led her to the deck where dinner would be served, at a small, square table laid with candles underneath the stars. It was a heavenly night, and they were far enough away from the shore now for the stars to play in all their glory. There wasn't another boat in sight.

Sheikh Ashraf stood looking out over the black, moon-spangled water. He turned as she stepped out into the semi-darkness. He had changed into a short-sleeved shirt and cotton pants. He could wear both Western and Eastern clothes with equal ease, she saw, and thought that he would make an excellent sultan. Fully at home in both East and West. He would understand where both sides were coming from.

"Wine?" Ashraf asked her. "Or a cocktail?"

"Wine," she agreed. "And some ice in it, please."

The manservant handed her the glass and then slipped away, leaving them alone together with the night and the stars. There was silence and then another track of music started, a wailing, haunting woman's voice.

Dana sipped her wine and realized that it was a very expensive one, and that watering it down with ice was probably a terrible insult to it. But she wanted a clear head tonight. The air was heavy with unspoken meaning.

"Was Prince Wafiq your father?" she asked, when they had stood in silence for a few minutes gazing into the darkness. She turned and leaned back against the railing, her glass resting on it at her side, her elbows back.

"He was."

"Yours and Harry's."

He inclined his head.

"Does Ghasib know that you were the one named as your grandfather's heir?"

It was obvious to her now that Sheikh Ashraf was the one named by his grandfather as Crown Prince-designate of Bagestan. She should have realized it the moment she noticed the family resemblance between the three men this afternoon, but it was only later, when Ashraf said Harry was his brother, that the penny had finally dropped. Amongst the Bagestani expat community, Prince Wafiq was widely rumoured to have had two sons. And Dana had finally clicked on why Naj looked familiar—his recent romantic reunion with his wife and son had been all over television and the papers. He had been revealed as Najib al Makhtoum, Hafzuddin al Jawadi's grandson.

So she had been talking to the three grandsons. There could be no doubt that Ashraf was the leader among them. His authority, both in himself and with the other two, was unmistakable. They had consistently deferred to him.

"We don't know for a certainty what Ghasib knows, or guesses, about us. But since the storytelling, we have to assume that he has come to the correct conclusion."

"That would be why they put the screws on Roxy the next morning," Dana guessed, and he nodded.

A servant arrived with a tray, and they sat down at the table. They were served with a beautifully presented starter of roasted vegetables, and at a sign from the sheikh were left alone to enjoy it.

"This is delicious!" Dana said, for once in her life finding silence unnerving. "Is your chef Bagestani?"

"By birth, but he was raised in Paris and trained there," Sheikh Ashraf said. They talked about food, and then about Bagestani culture and what had happened to it over the past three decades. The meal progressed, and each course seemed more spectacular than the last.

But Dana couldn't quite relax. The subject they did not speak of hovered over the conversation. What did he want of her, and what would it entail?

"Do you like the sea? Are you a good sailor?" he

asked her at last, when little cups of Turkish coffee had been served, and a plate of bite-sized morsels of fresh fruit in the centre of the table was all that remained of the meal.

"I haven't done all that much sailing. I like boats, yes. Why?"

"I wondered if you would enjoy a holiday at sea."

"Is that what you want me to do? Stay aboard?"

The breeze was warm but gusting strongly now, and the candle flames were caught by it, even inside the protective globes. Ash looked at her in the flickering darkness and wished she were less beautiful. Or that he could send her away till it was over rather than do what he had to—ask her to stay in close proximity.

"We may gain something, as Harry said, if Fuad al Kadthib and his partner believe you to be successfully obeying orders," he told her. "If they have assassination in mind, they may see you as a possible means. If it is disgrace that they plan, again, they can't hope to send in another woman when you are with me."

"Starting when?"

"Effectively, now. Tonight it will be best, I think, if you return to the Eden Roc. In the morning you can check out. For you to simply disappear and have strangers collect your luggage will attract too much attention."

"And then what?"

"We do not know where Ghasib's spies are, or how much he knows. It would not be good enough for you merely to say you are with me. You would have to be actually with me here."

"You mean, to convince them that I'm in position and can be activated whenever they choose," Dana said flatly.

He bent his head.

Dana was furious suddenly. "And what do I say when they give me a vial of poison to feed you, or ask me to take you to such and such a place so they can use you for target practice? What if they trick me? What if they've already tricked me? What if there's a bomb in my suitcase or a...an inhalant poison in my perfume or something?"

He looked at her. *Not poison, but intoxication,* he thought. *And just as dangerous to my concentration.*

"These are mostly unfounded fears," he told her gently.

"I—"

"And they can be counteracted by a thorough examination of your luggage before you bring it aboard. What arrangement did you make with these men for contacting them?"

"None. I'm supposed to keep in touch with Roxy. I have no idea how often she talks to them. Too often, probably."

"Suppose you phone your sister tonight and tell her that I have invited you to stay with me at a secret location. Do not mention the *Dhikra,* or let her know that you are at sea at all. Say that the phone will be monitored where you are going and you will not call her again for a week or more, but that after that time I have promised to take you to Paris and London."

"On a shopping trip," she suggested, one corner of her mouth tilting.

Ashraf laughed, getting the joke at once. "On a shopping trip," he agreed. "Tell her that your rich Arab lover has promised to deck your beauty in the precious jewels it deserves."

His voice roughened at the end, as if he had started out joking and then lost his grip. Their eyes met for a moment over the candle flames, and her pulse raced as if his gaze were a physical touch.

"Roxy will love that," she said, for something to say.

"And you, Dana—what do you love?" he asked. The words seemed to come from him unwillingly, and her heart responded with even more wild thudding. Before she could answer, his lips tightened and he dragged his eyes away from her. "I apologize," he said.

"What?"

"I want you to feel secure with me, Dana. If you agree to these plans, do not be afraid that I will be unable to keep to my part of the bargain."

"Which is—what?" Dana said, her heart choking her.

"You are a beautiful, deeply attractive woman. In the nature of things we must be often alone together while you are here. But I will not take advantage of this situation, or your cooperation."

Dana pressed her lips together, wondering how to answer this. At last she asked, "Are you married?"

His eyes narrowed at her. After a moment he said slowly, "I am not married. No."

"Engaged? Involved?"

Ash saw the direction of her thoughts. He shook his head protestingly, closing his eyes. Took a deep breath.

"Dana..." he began.

"Who told you that I wanted to be protected from you?" she asked softly. "Or haven't you noticed that you are also handsome and deeply attractive?"

"Dana," he said, in a different voice, shoved his chair back and stood. He looked at her with eyes that were as black and as deep as the sky behind his head.

Ten

He drew her to her feet and wrapped his arms securely around her back. She lifted her own arms around his neck, and they stood there for a moment, with the music playing softly around them, gazing into each other's face. A thousand wordless messages seemed to pass between them.

Her blood took heat from his body, so that she was burning up from the inside. The touch of his mouth was electric on her lips, brushing softly, softly over the fullness till she was crazy for the firm pressure of hunger. She understood that she had been waiting for this every moment since that first kiss.

His hunger at last grew too much for him, and he pressed one hand into her hair, cupping her head and turning her chin helplessly up before his mouth came down with a loss of control that thrilled her to her bones.

His arms tightened almost painfully, drawing her

against his body. Blood thundered in her ears and brain, drowning out the soft music, making her dizzy. She opened her mouth to his, hungrier than she had ever been for a man, and her hands pressed his neck and tangled in his hair. Of its own volition her body arched into his, responsive to the pressure of his demanding hands, making demands of its own.

His hands were inside her shirt, slipping underneath her tank top, his skin rough and warm against her bare skin. She trembled and melted at the incredible intimacy of the touch.

He drew his mouth away and they gazed into the magical night in each other's dark eyes. She was meltingly, wildly hungry for him. He bent to press his lips against her throat and she closed her eyes and felt herself half-fainting. Her blood thundered in her ears, and she saw light behind her eyelids, and suddenly Ashraf's hands gripped her upper arms and she was being held away from his warmth.

"You drive me to the edge," he muttered.

The clamour in her blood abated, but the swooping thunder was still in her ears. Dana understood suddenly, and with a little gasp looked up.

The helicopter, its bright searchlight beaming down, was slowly lowering onto the deck above their heads. She stared at it uncomprehendingly for a moment, and then said huskily, "Is that for me?"

Ashraf drew back out of her arms, set her away from him. "To take you back to the hotel," he said. "There is someone to accompany you. Sharif Azad al Dauleh. He will examine your luggage, and assist you wherever necessary. Tomorrow he will bring you back again."

She brushed the back of one hand over her kiss-swollen lips. "All right," she said. He had better control than she did—she didn't think she would have been able to pull back from the brink like that for any money.

"I guess you don't get to be considered sultan material without a larger than usual dose of self-discipline," she muttered.

"Not as much as I need," he said roughly.

She supposed he had chewed her lipstick all over her face. She turned to reach for her handbag, on a lounge chair. The helicopter was just touching down on the upper deck, and she knew she should be up there already. The pilot had explained to her on the way in how tricky such a landing was.

"Good night," she said tonelessly, tossing the bag over her shoulder as she crossed to the stairs.

He said nothing as he followed her up to the top deck. He bent double and ran towards the chopper, and she followed suit.

"Till tomorrow," he said, when she had clambered into the empty seat and strapped herself in, and that was all they had time for. He bent and ran back the way he had come, and the helicopter lifted off. A moment later the brightly lighted yacht was only a shape in the surrounding sea of blackness.

"Oh, you are so lucky!" Roxy's voice came enviously down the wire.

"I've got a sister with a very short memory, if you call that luck," Dana responded. Roxy seemed to have wiped recent events from her mind. She was reacting a little as though Dana had stolen some excitement that was rightfully hers.

"Don't tell me you're not enjoying yourself. I wouldn't believe you!" she accused.

"Snap!"

"What does that mean?" Roxy demanded petulantly.

"You enjoy pulling strings and manipulating people," Dana told her, suddenly seeing the truth of this herself clearly for the first time. "You especially have always enjoyed watching me bust my ass to pull things out of the fire that you have deliberately tossed in. And you're enjoying it now."

"I am *not*. I don't know how you can say that, Dana!"

"I can say it because it's true."

"It is not!"

"Then listen up, and stop oohing and aahing as if you think that if it weren't for me you'd be here playing footsie with a sheikh yourself. If it weren't for me, you'd be explaining to Dad why you felt the thrill of a few hours' gambling was worth everything he's worked for in life and then some."

Roxy subsided into sullen silence. But for once, she wasn't sure why, Dana wasn't impressed. Maybe it was the contrast: she had sensed a ruthless self-honesty in Ashraf Durran, and it was a deeply attractive trait. She was sure he was a man who never tried to blind himself as to his own motives.

The problem with people who played games with themselves was that, if you loved them, you ended up playing the games too. You sold out the truth to soothe them.

And maybe that was what had enabled Roxy to go on in the irresponsible path she had apparently chosen in life. Dana had not only fixed things for her, but had always reassured her that what she had done wasn't very important in the scheme of things.

Who did she have to blame if it had now come to

this—Roxy, believing she had forced her sister into prostitution, was now pretending to envy her.

"Tell them I am going away with Sheikh Durran," Dana said concisely. "He hasn't said where, only that we'll be there a week or so. And then he'll bring me back to London and Paris. I won't call you again till we arrive in London, because we'll be somewhere I can't use the phone."

She didn't say anything about having told the sheikh the truth. Roxy just couldn't be trusted to carry it off if she knew. But Dana would have loved to be able to ask her sister if she knew of any reason why Sheikh Durran should have offered to pay off the full amount Roxy owed, no questions asked.

Sharif Azad al Dauleh checked every inch of her luggage and pronounced it clean, and by eleven the next morning was escorting her back to the *Dhikra* by helicopter. It was a longer ride than last night's, so the yacht must have been sailing through the night.

Dana had phoned no one except Roxy. Mostly she was comfortable with this, but from time to time she was struck by doubt. Gut instinct told her Sheikh Ashraf Durran was a man to be trusted. Logic warned her that she might be mistaken. What if she sailed off with him and never returned? Would Roxy be believed if she told her story?

In the end she had gone to the hotel's cyber café, briefly noted the facts and sent the document to her own e-mail address. No one else had her password, but she supposed that if she went missing the police would get it soon enough. And that would have to do.

The sheikh was not there to meet her when she arrived on board. A stewardess showed Dana to a different stateroom than the one she had borrowed last night. It was a suite consisting of sitting room, bath and bedroom with two huge empty closets, and a small study with a computer and several shelves of books.

Most of the books were worn with use, but one shelf was filled with what looked like new purchases. Dana scanned the titles and saw that they were a mix of recently published literary and popular books, and some classics. A biography of Byron sat side by side with half a dozen paperback romances and the latest John Grisham. There was a history of Bagestan.

A smile pulled the corners of her mouth as she noticed a beautiful Moroccan leather-bound four-volume set. *The Complete Works of William Shakespeare. Comedies. Histories. Tragedies. Poems and Sonnets.*

So he had not just said, *Get her a few books to keep her from boredom.* He had thought about one, at least.

"Where is Sheikh Ashraf?" she asked the stewardess, a Frenchwoman named Adile who told Dana that she had come aboard early this morning.

"He is in a meeting in the boardroom, madame," she replied.

"A meeting?"

"With some men who flew in an hour ago," Adile explained. "His Excellency asks that you excuse him. They will take lunch together in the large dining room. And when would you like your own lunch to be served, madame?"

So she wasn't going to be asked to act as his hostess, Dana understood with a little pang of disappointment. Then she told herself she was being a fool. Why should she be?

A few minutes later, wearing a tankini swimsuit under a matching knee-length green shirt, her hair tied back

with its own knot, Dana went out to the aft deck for a
bottle of water. She found one of the deckhands there,
snipping the wires off the thick stack of newspapers that
had been dropped off by the helicopter pilot. There were
two copies of everything, and the deckhand was dividing
them into two piles. When he had finished, he pulled the
old papers out of the newspaper rack and slipped one
new stack in. He tossed the old papers down behind the
serving bar before disappearing inside with the second
stack of new ones.

Dana paused to glance through the headlines. There
were several of today's English broadsheets, as well as
yesterday afternoon's tabloids, papers from France, Ger-
many, Italy and elsewhere in Europe, and one or two of
yesterday's papers from North America.

Al Jawadi Flings Down The Gauntlet, cried one splash
headline on a Canadian paper. Dana suddenly realized
that she had missed yesterday's reporting of the Night
of the Thousand and One Books and went and retrieved
the papers from behind the bar.

"Madame?"

It was the drinks waiter, who appeared a little ruffled,
not having realized she was out here.

Message To Ghasib—Get Out! one of the tabloids
screamed. Dana glanced up at the waiter with a preoc-
cupied smile. "May I have a bottle of mineral water to
take up to the pool with me?" she asked.

He frowned at her. "You go to pool? Swimmink?"
He made motions for the sake of clarity.

"Yeah," Dana said lightly. She had picked up an ol-
ive from a bowl behind the bar and was absently munch-
ing it.

Are You Our Sultan?

"You go up, we brink," the man told her sternly. He pointed to the intercom on the bar. "You say what."

"Well, I'm here now," Dana began, then gave up. His English wasn't good enough for an explanation— she would just confuse him. "All right, mineral water and lime, then, please."

She had to wait while he laboriously showed her two bottles, and she pointed to the sparkling variety. Then, tucking several papers, new and old, under her arm, Dana made her way up to the swimming pool and sank into a comfortable lounger under a striped umbrella.

It was heaven. The sea stretched for miles around, a beautiful, empty blue.

She was followed a few minutes later by Adile, bearing a tray with a bottle of water in an ice bucket, a tub of ice, a glass, a plate of sliced lime, and several bowls of tidbits. She arranged everything neatly on the little table beside Dana's lounger.

"Anything else, madame?" she asked, straightening.

Dana smiled at her. "Thanks, that's fine. Adile, why did you bring this up, instead of Abdulahad?"

"Because I am your personal maid, madame. I have been instructed by His Excellency to look after you personally in everything, as far as possible."

She sounded as though death would have to intervene before she defaulted on her sworn duty, and Dana, hearing the hero worship behind the tone, thought that with charisma like this Ashraf couldn't possibly fail.

"I see. Well, thank you," she said, a bit helplessly.

Adile nodded and left her to the perusal of the papers.

Where Is Our Sultan?

Several papers had photographs of the demonstrations taking place in Medinat al Bostan, the capital of Bagestan. According to the story, it was illegal in Bagestan to congregate for the purposes of political discussion, and Ghasib routinely punished any infraction with extreme measures. It was also illegal for crowds to gather in front of Ghasib's grotesque New Palace.

So the demonstrations were taking place in the city's central square in front of the elegant Old Palace—which had once been the home of the al Jawadis—and they had been completely silent.

Dana gasped when she read that. Thousands of people standing silently together for hours—what a will they must have! They deserved Ashraf as a sultan. No lesser man would do.

She swam and read, and ate a late lunch where she was, and wondered how long he would be stuck in his meeting, and when he would be free to come to her. She dozed and dreamed of him, and awoke and read more journalists' informed guesses as to whether Sheikh Ashraf Durran was himself the sultan-in-waiting, or merely his messenger.

It is widely believed that, when the sultan-designate announces himself publicly, he will produce the al Jawadi Rose—the fabulous sixty-three-carat pink diamond ring that has been passed from the reigning sultan to his designated successor for generations.

The jewel is a potent symbol for most Bagestanis, even though it has not been seen by anyone outside the family since Prince Nazim was named Crown Prince thirty-three years ago. The belief has been given great impetus by Sheikh Ashraf Durran's clear mention of the Rose during his remarkable performance at the Cannes charity function.

She dozed again and woke to the noise of the helicopter's landing. She watched as several men in crumpled summer suits clambered aboard and it took off again, leaving the sheikh standing on the landing pad. The chopper dropped quickly astern as it climbed. Ashraf turned, saw her on the lounger and came towards her.

Her thighs melted with anticipation, and her blood came suddenly alive. She felt both electrically alive and lazily sensuous at the same time.

"Good afternoon," he said, as Dana swung her long legs off the lounger and sat up, pulling on her shirt.

"Isn't it, though?" she agreed with a smile. "Can I pour you something to drink?" She had long ago asked Adile to bring a second glass up. She scooped some half-melted ice cubes into it and drew the dripping bottle of water out of the ice bucket.

"Thank you," he said after a beat, and sank down into a chair opposite her. He was wearing Western clothes today—casual, loose-fitting trousers in navy cotton with a neat braided belt, a white polo-neck shirt, and bare feet in deck shoes. His skin looked clean and healthy, his hair glowed. His chin was dark with beard shadow, which only made him sexier.

She passed him the glass, offered him the bowl of olives, watched in satisfaction as he took a long drink and popped a couple of the green globes into his mouth.

"How did your meeting go?"

He lifted his shoulders, getting the kinks out. "Long-winded, but about as productive as could be expected."

"Who were they?"

"Representatives of a multinational which has an established presence in Bagestan. They naturally want to be reassured that they are not going to be the losers if Ghasib goes.''

''What does that mean?''

''They won't want to see me on the throne if it means their profits are reduced.''

''And you have to reassure them?''

One eyebrow went up, and he drank again. ''Yes, and no. On the one hand they have a very sweet deal with Ghasib—he gives them pretty wide latitude in return for their support. On the other hand, they have lately been getting flak back home because of their collusion with his regime, and it's becoming harder and harder for them to pretend they aren't involved in the atrocities against protesters and the wanton environmental pollution.

''They can only threaten me at the moment, because they know that if it were proven that they were actively conspiring to keep Ghasib in power their share price would drop. And they can't be sure that I don't have the evidence.''

She was sickened. ''I can't believe you have to do deals with people like that!''

He gestured at a newspaper folded open on the photo of a demonstration. ''The more the people of Bagestan go out on the streets, the less I'll have to compromise— with everyone. But I have no genie in a bottle. Nothing happens in a vacuum, not even the sultan riding in on his white horse.''

She saw suddenly how tired he was, how sick of dealing with people who thought of nothing but their profits. ''Are you finished for the day?'' she asked.

He shook his head. ''I have briefing papers to read in advance of another meeting tomorrow.'' He looked at his watch. ''And the helicopter will bring back our public relations advisor.''

"Have a swim first," she urged him. "It's so hot and the pool's lovely and cool."

"I have been in an air-conditioned room," he pointed out humorously.

"Take a break," she pleaded.

And suddenly the air between them was singing with meaning. Sensation rushed over her skin, so that she shivered in the heat.

Ashraf watched her without speaking for a pregnant moment, dropped his eyes to his glass, lifted it and finished the water in it.

"*Baleh,*" he said. He slipped out of his shoes where he sat, pulled his polo shirt out of his pants and over his head. She watched the tanned skin emerge, firm with muscle, and almost fainted with the rush of desire that assailed her. His forearms and his chest were dark with hair.

He stood up, his hands going to his belt, and for one crazy moment, thinking he was going to strip and swim naked, she felt her heart stop. But he was wearing a neat pair of swim trunks. He stepped over to the edge of the pool and dived neatly in.

Dana slipped out of her own shirt. She was wearing a dark green tankini top with a thong. The outfit suited her long, neatly muscled body, the small, firm breasts, her skin all a pale mocha shade. She kicked off green sandals and followed Ashraf into the pool.

It wasn't a large pool, ten metres long at most, not something you could get a real workout in. But it was cooling and relaxing, and best of all, filled with sea water, so she didn't have to worry about chlorine on her hair.

Dhikra's colours were dark green and navy. There were stacks of towels in these colours on a cart beside the freshwater shower at one side of the pool. When he had done a dozen quick lengths, Ashraf pulled himself out and rinsed down in the shower before grabbing a towel.

He turned to see Dana coming towards him, water beaded on her long, slender body, her breasts tight under her top, the thong clinging to her mound, outlining the thickly curling hair. She had slim, straight shoulders, smoothly curved arms, a dancer's muscled legs, a neat rump. She passed him, stroking the salt water from her eyelashes, and stepped under the shower. He felt a wave of psychic heat as she went past.

The sun was hot. The air was perfumed—either by the flowering plants on the deck below, or by her passing, he did not know which. In the shower she was turning her face up to the spray exactly as she had lifted her mouth for his kiss last night.

Ashraf turned, slung the towel around his neck, strode to the other end of the deck and went down the stairs.

Eleven

She didn't see him again until dinner, when he introduced her to Gazi al Hamzeh, his public relations advisor. They ate on deck again, under the stars. Ashraf was very silent, and Gazi did most of the talking, explaining to Dana how a public relations campaign was managed.

"So basically you're saying you could make anybody at all famous for nothing at all," she laughed.

For dinner she had dressed in a rose red raw silk dress that was slim and sleeveless, with a high Japanese collar. It fell below the knee, slit for a couple of inches on each side seam. Her hair was clipped casually up on top of her head with diamanté clips.

"Not literally anybody, but close enough," he said. "Even twenty years ago it wouldn't have been all that difficult, but today?" Gazi waved a hand.

She was interested, but her interest was given focus

by her determination to suppress her response to Ashraf's presence. And he seemed determined to all but ignore her.

"Would you like the treatment?" Gazi asked.

She grinned. "You're offering to make me a celebrity?"

"In England, of course, you already are. It would be an easy thing to spread the word and make you more of a name internationally. It could boost your career."

Still smiling, she shook her head.

"Why not? Consider it our thank-you for coming to Ashraf with the truth."

"I don't particularly like addictive substances," she said. Gazi raised his eyebrows, and she gestured at her glass of wine. "Like alcohol, a little fame goes a long way. It's one thing if it comes as a by-product of something I've achieved. It would be another thing completely if it were the result of nothing more than media manipulation."

Gazi laughed as if she had won a point. He had an attractive birthmark patch all around one eye. He looked like a pirate, and she thought that, in some ways, he was one.

"You and my wife would get along," he said. "You'd like her."

She saw Ashraf watching her with dark eyes, but the expression in them was unreadable.

The helicopter came to take Gazi away, and as usual, Ashraf went up to the landing pad to see him off. He returned to where Dana was sitting, his steps slow, and she heard reluctance in the tread. Her heart contracted with sadness, because what could it mean except that he did not, after all, find her as attractive as she found him?

Part of her cried that he did. He must. How was it she

could feel so much, so quickly, if he did not feel an answering passion? It wasn't possible!

She had moved from the dining table to a lounger, and was sitting with her feet up looking out over the stern, watching the helicopter's lights disappear, watching starlight flicker and break on *Dhikra*'s wake.

She felt him pause behind her, but did not turn her head. *Don't let him go,* she begged. *Let him stay with me.*

He moved silently past her to stand at the rail. For a moment he stood looking out over the black sea. The moon hadn't risen. There was no visible horizon line, just a depth of star-speckled darkness.

He turned, and she felt his movement brush her, though he was at a distance of five feet. "Dana," he said.

She closed her eyes, for the tone in his voice was not the one she wanted to hear. It was the voice of a man who was going to tell her why he couldn't love her.

She sighed and opened her eyes again. There was a little wine left in her glass, and she drained it and leaned over to set the empty glass on a table. Resting her elbows on the arms of the chair, she folded her hands over her abdomen.

"All right," she said.

"Dana, you know what work I have ahead of me. I don't think I have to argue with you over its importance, as we did in London, because I know now you didn't really believe what you said that night. I think you accept that what we plan is vital to the lives and happiness of many more than ourselves."

The last thing she had expected him to broach tonight was politics. A kind of disappointed fury shook her. Did he really not understand what she was feeling?

"And why is it important that I accept that?"

His eyes searched hers in the dark. "Dana, you could derail me. And if me, then the whole project."

She gasped. For a moment, neither spoke. Her surprise hung in the silence between them.

"I have never been so drawn to a woman, Dana. Never been so disturbed by a woman's presence."

Her heart protested with three heavy jolts. "Ashraf," she whispered.

"Let me finish. I know, or perhaps I desire it so much it feels like certainty, that you, too, are drawn to me. I think you believe, expect—that we should become lovers tonight."

His voice was like butterfly wings over her skin, causing shiver after shiver of sensation.

"My heart craves such a simple solution. My body begs for it."

"Then what—" she began, but broke off. Her voice was drowned in her own ears by the clamorous song of her blood.

"Dana, I can't do it. I am engaged in the most important endeavour of my life—the most important endeavour in three generations of my family's history. I have to remain focussed. I have to maintain a clear head. The smallest slip could bring disaster on us all. Do you understand?"

Since he had knocked her brain reeling with his first words, understanding wasn't exactly what she would call her state of mind at the moment. She swallowed.

"Um…" she tried. She licked her lips and tried again. "Uh—"

"I am out of my depth with you. If I allow myself to make love to you now I know that I will drown. You are not a woman whose bed a man leaves and forgets. You are—"

His throat closed and his voice grated to a halt.

"What am I?" she whispered.

"You said half an hour ago to Gazi that fame was an addictive substance. I look at you and I know that you are that to me, Dana. You have the potential to absorb my every waking thought. If I spent the next month nowhere else but in your bed it would be only the beginning. I knew it the first moment I set eyes on you. I knew nothing about you, except that I had met my destiny. A moment too soon."

She sobbed with reaction and relief and got to her feet. "Oh, Ashraf!" she whispered, reaching for him.

He could not resist her when her cheeks were wet with tears. Ashraf wrapped his arms savagely around her and took her mouth with a wildness that made them drunk. She entwined her hands in his hair and pressed him closer, as hunger for his closeness swamped her.

But when her body arched against him with deep, flooding yearning, he lifted his lips and, looking into her eyes, shook his head. Then he kissed her eyes with a gentleness that made more tears flow.

"I cannot do it without your cooperation," he murmured. "If you push me, now or in the days to come, I will crack, Dana."

"Well, then—"

"But I will regret it. Even as we make love my heart will whisper that I steal my own pleasure at the expense of the happiness of many. I do not want guilt to lie between us in the bed, Dana. I ask you to accept my decision. We will not have to wait long."

Faced with that, what argument could she muster? She thought he was wrong, she was convinced he was only making things harder on himself. How she would love to wrap her arms around him and convince him she was right! But the choice had to be his. He was only suggesting a delay in their pleasures, after all. And she had to accept that he knew himself better than she did.

She lifted her hand to his cheek and smiled. "Delaying gratification is supposed to be a sign of maturity, and now I know why," she said ruefully.

She felt the tension go out of him, and realized that he had feared her opposition. He caught her hand in his and kissed the palm, then straightened and set her away from him.

"I will do my best to make it up to you," he said, with a lazy, promising smile that took her already overheated blood up another couple of degrees. They walked back to the table.

"I am going to have coffee while I work," Ash said. "Will you have some with me?"

She wished she could help him. "Is there anything I can do? Who's on the agenda for tomorrow?"

"There is nothing you can do, except to sit with me while I work. Tomorrow we have a meeting with the oil company executives."

"Oh! Are they on your side?"

He looked at her. "They are on the side of their profits, in Bagestan as anywhere, Dana. What do they care about national politics? They financed Ghasib's coup against my grandfather thirty years ago because my grandfather stood up to them, refusing to let them take all the profits out of the country. They only look to me because they know that Ghasib's power base is eroding and they are more afraid of the Islamic militants than of me."

"Do you need them to succeed?"

He lifted both hands in an eloquent shrug. "Who knows what we need or don't need? We are trying to hold off from all firm commitments, especially with these villains. But I do not dare to show my hand too soon. If the oil companies actively moved against us—"

Abdulahad arrived with more Turkish coffee. Ashraf flicked on a reading light, lifted a briefcase onto a small side table, opened it, chose a thick document, and sank into one of the loungers. Dana went to her suite, collected the Bagestan history book from the shelf there, and came back on deck.

Conquest to Coup: The History of Bagestan from Cyrus the Great to President Ghasib. Dana settled on a lounger beside Ashraf's and cracked the cover. It looked very densely written. She glanced over at him, and sensing her eyes on him, he looked up.

"You are sure that this is the way you want it?" she asked, with a rueful grimace.

He only gave her a look that melted her bones, shook his head a little, and turned back to business.

For the next two days she hardly saw him. There were others staying on the yacht now, his brother and cousin among them, and although she dined with them in the evenings, there was no small talk. It was all business.

She spent the hot, lazy days reading by the pool while the helicopter came and went and the meetings went on and on. The newspapers, particularly the English and Italian tabloids, were getting daily more excited about the subject of Bagestan's "Sultan-in-Hiding." They speculated, they agonized, they recapped history, all in a bid to blind the reader to the fact that they had no firm evidence as to who the sultan was, and not an idea in hell where to find him.

One paper ran a murky photo of a palatial, if unidentifiable, building, and suggested that the sultan-in-waiting was holding his meetings there. Another hinted that he was actually within the borders of Bagestan, very dangerously, waiting to lead an uprising.

Ghasib, meanwhile, was reported to have gone to ground inside the hideous New Palace compound. Dana wondered where he really was. Meanwhile, one thing was certain—the silent protests were growing larger by the hour, were extending into all-night vigils, and neither the army nor the police were moving to break them up.

On the second night, as on the previous one, Ash, his brother, Haroun, their cousin Najib, Gazi al Hamzeh, Prince Omar and a couple of assistants sat discussing the day just past, and the one to come.

"It's my feeling we can get away with a very light nod on the alcohol question," Ashraf said, and the others agreed. "A ban on actual alcohol production within the country I think would do it, in addition to what's already in place. What do we have in production in the country? How many jobs would a ban affect?"

Someone pulled out a sheet of statistics and they discussed how the businesses affected could be protected.

"But it looks like we're going to run aground on the *hejab* question."

Dana, who by this time had left the table and was on a lounger, reading, with her back to them, pricked up her ears. *Hejab* meant veil. It meant women covering their hair according to Islamic rules.

"I don't think they're going to give way on that."

"Well, let's give it another try. It would be a very unpopular move. Who's closest to compromise there?"

They were speaking in English half the time and Bagestani Arabic the other half, and Dana found it very difficult to follow the thread. If they had settled into Arabic she might have got her bearings, but the constant switch confused her ear.

"They have to see how difficult a curfew is to police...."

When the discussion was over at last and they were refreshing their coffees and slipping into ordinary conversation, Dana got up and slowly approached the table. They all looked up as she sank into her vacant seat.

"Who's coming tomorrow?" She reached for the coffee pot and poured herself another cup.

"The *ulema* are due for another round of argument," Ash told her dryly.

The *ulema* were the religious leaders in Bagestan.

"Do you have their support?" she asked.

He rubbed the back of his neck. "The extreme leaders of course will not back me, they're behind the Islamic movement. The moderates coming in the morning have—like the multinationals—got to the point of demanding concessions from us."

Although he had turned the Central Mosque into a museum, Ghasib had not completely suppressed religion in Bagestan, Dana knew. But there was total separation of mosque and state. No religious precept was enshrined in the law of the nation. What Ashraf was telling her was that the mullahs were hoping to force him to change that.

"And are you going to give in?"

"On as few points as possible."

"Are you going to give in on the question of *hejab?*" she pressed, stirring her coffee.

"Not unless we absolutely have to," Ash said.

"What does that mean—absolutely have to? You're

talking about the freedom of half your subjects. Why would you *have* to compromise their rights?''

They were all watching her now.

Gazi said, ''I understand your concerns, Dana, but Ashraf has got to get some religious leaders behind him. However moderate they are, the vast majority of the citizens are Muslim, and if the mullahs start preaching against Ashraf now...it could be critical.''

''So after thirty years of a dictator, the men of Bagestan will be free, but the women will just switch to a different kind of oppression,'' she said levelly.

''We are working on it,'' Ash said. ''Of course we don't want—''

She interrupted him without apology. ''It was your grandfather who created the separation of mosque and state,'' she reminded him, having just learned this fact from the history book she had been reading. ''Not Ghasib. Hafzuddin made all the women in his government abandon the veil. He let women run for parliament. He started with those reforms almost fifty years ago.''

''Times change, Dana.''

''Do they? I don't think so,'' she snapped. ''Not when it comes to women. People always complain that religion oppresses women, but it's not really religion, is it? It's men! Men will pick up any handy tool and use it to beat women down! Religion is just a convenient tool.''

''I am not using religion or any other tool to beat women down,'' Ash said stiffly.

'''Women hold up half the sky'—who said that?''

''I don't know,'' Ash said stiffly.

''Chairman Mao,'' Harry supplied.

''Right! About fifty years ago. And who said this one—'women are the twin-halves of men'?''

They all knew. ''Dana...''

"The Prophet Mohammad," she told them anyway. "Fourteen hundred years ago. Is anybody listening yet?"

"Dana, in a situation like this we can't act exactly the way we want to, or even the way we should. It's just a—"

"If you don't act the way you should, Ashraf, how are you different from Ghasib? If you're prepared to sell out women in order to gain power, what does that say about you? Who are you liberating from Ghasib's yoke? Women as well as men are counting on you, as I am sure you know.

"Look at the photographs in the papers—at least half of the people who are staging the demonstrations that you're counting on to bring you to power are women. You're going to imprison those women further in order to free the men. What kind of sultan will you make if that's the kind of 'freedom' you bring?"

They all sat silent and uncomfortable, looking at her or into their coffee cups. "Dana, nothing's perfect in this world. I will do my best, but—" He left it hanging.

Dana shook her head in disgust, shoved her cup away from her, stood, and left them.

She was so angry she thought she would explode. She arrived back in her stateroom and slammed the door in a bid to release her feelings, but it didn't have much effect.

She was angriest because she loved him and admired him, and this proved him to have clay feet up to the hips. She couldn't believe he had said what she'd heard him say. The same tired old arguments that had been used for decades.

She had been right the first time she'd set eyes on him. Ashraf al Jawadi was a man just like her father.

Twelve

She made no attempt to join them for breakfast in the dining room next morning, instead waiting until she heard the helicopter arrive with the mullahs and then going to the aft deck for a solitary breakfast.

She rubbed her head where a headache was just settling in behind her temples. She hadn't slept well last night; she was drinking too much coffee too late at night, she told herself. And crying herself to sleep didn't help.

After breakfast, as was becoming her habit, Dana took a few of the newly arrived papers and a book and went up to the pool.

But she couldn't settle. The bloom had gone off the situation. She had not minded the enforced idleness over the past couple of days because she felt she was at least contributing to good. What did she have to console her now? Ashraf was down there selling out the women of Bagestan to men whose whole sense of self-importance seemed to derive from telling others how to behave, how to live their religion.

The day was long and tedious. She swam a little, but without much satisfaction. A few strokes and she was at the other end of the pool. And then the Med got choppy, and the water started slapping around in the pool as the yacht negotiated the waves.

As the sea got rougher, Dana wondered how they were managing in the boardroom. Ashraf and the others on his team were experienced sailors, but she doubted if the mullahs were. As if in response to her thoughts, Dana felt the engines slow and went to the railing to look out forward.

They were approaching a small island, with a beautiful half-moon bay. Several other boats were also seeking refuge there, and she soon saw why. Once inside the arms of the half-moon, the water became tranquil again.

She had no idea where they were or what country the island belonged to. She watched as the anchor went down, and then there was silence as the engines were shut off.

This was her first chance to swim in the Med itself, and, her shirt billowing behind her, Dana went quickly down the staircase to ask one of the deckhands to lower the ladder. Pausing only to take a towel, she went down to the landing platform, stripped off her beach shirt, and dived in.

The water was fabulous—clear, clean, a rich blue-green. The island had sandstone cliffs, and one or two tiny islands of sandstone punctured the water of the bay closer in to shore. She struck out for one of them, her body grateful for the freedom after her days of confinement.

She landed on the first rock. Sandstone had been harvested from it at some time in the past, and it still retained the shape of the building blocks that had been removed from it. She swam on to the next and then saw snorkellers a short distance away, trawling back and forth over a confined area, and swam to take a look. But instead of the coral bed she half expected, what met her eyes was an underwater ruin—a sunken city.

Dana headed back to the yacht, where she was supplied with a snorkel and flippers, and spent the next hour contentedly swimming over the remains of the underwater rooms of the long-dead city. Late in the day she saw the helicopter arrive to take the mullahs off, and she headed back to the yacht. She wondered if the mullahs had got their way. She wondered if Ashraf would tell her.

She was sitting at the dressing table wearing only her beach shirt, brushing the day's tangles from her hair, when she heard a second helicopter arrive and depart. Ashraf's team must be leaving for the night, too. A moment later, just as the yacht's engines were starting up, there was a knock on her door. Not Adile's gentle tap, but the strong, firm rap of impatient knuckles.

She turned in her chair, brush in hand, and gazed at the door for a moment, with a slight sense of foreboding. "Come in," she cried.

Ashraf opened the door and stepped inside, looking very Bagestani in a kaftan and *keffiyeh*. No doubt he had put them on to make the mullahs feel at home.

She couldn't help the smile that came to her lips when she saw him, angry though she might be. She got to her feet and stepped towards him as he entered and closed the door.

Then his eyes moved to meet hers, but his gaze was

not a friendly one. It was black with anger and disapproval. Dana stopped where she was, halfway across the room from him, feeling she had hit a stone wall.

"Ashraf!"

He crossed his arms and stood looking at her. "What did you hope to gain by today's display, Dana?"

She blinked uncomprehendingly. "What?"

"Did you just want to make us all acutely uncomfortable, or were you hoping to sabotage today's talks completely?"

"What on *earth* are you talking about?"

He pointed at her body. "I am talking about you running around the yacht all but naked in full view of the boardroom windows. You knew who we were in discussion with today, so don't tell me it was an accident. It was deliberate, and I would like to know what you hoped to achieve!"

"All but naked?" Dana's fury, never slow to ignite, erupted with an engulfing swoosh. "Who do you think you're talking to?" she cried. "Don't you speak to me in that tone of voice! You're not sultan yet, and even if you were I wouldn't accept that from you!"

"I think I'm talking to someone who puts her own opinion above everyone else's, whatever is at stake!" he said, in a low, gravelly voice. "Whether you want to accept it from me or not, I'm here to tell you that today's display was an outrage. You know perfectly well the mullahs are deeply religious men who—"

"Who what?" she demanded. "Who what, Ash? Who can't look at a woman's legs without their passions becoming ignited by the sight? What kind of crap is that? They can see naked women on *billboards!* What do they do about that?"

"Billboards are one thing. On my yacht is something

else. Is it asking too much of you to dress more appro-
priately when such men are my guests?''

She stared at him, her pulse beating in her throat, her
temples. ''I am not in a mosque, Ash, or even the middle
of a city,'' she said levelly. ''I am on a boat in the
Mediterranean, and I was swimming. My dress is *entirely* appropriate to that. A lot of women would have
been topless. I didn't realize that I could be seen from
the boardroom. I don't even know where the boardroom
is. But if I had known, it wouldn't have occurred to me
to button my shirt to spare the blushes of men who, after
all, are supposed to have had some training and experience in self-control. If it bothered them to see me, why
didn't you offer them blindfolds?''

''What?'' he exploded, outraged.

''If they didn't like seeing my body, why is that *my*
problem? It's *their* problem!'' she expounded, stabbing
the air with a forefinger. ''So let them deal with it. The
one solution men always come up with when there's a
question of men not being able to control their passions
is that *women* should be forced to correct this weakness.
Women should hide. Why don't they ever think that if a
man is so weak he can't control himself, he *ought to be
forced to wear a blindfold?*''

''You're being—''

''Or isn't it a question of men's unbridled passions at
all? Is it maybe just an excuse for exerting control over
women? Well, I am not going to give in to that, for your
sake or anyone else's. I was born a free citizen of a free
country. Don't ever think you're going to take that away
from me without a battle.''

''I am not trying to take away your freedom! But—''

''You *are!* Not only my freedom of the person, but
my freedom of religion! *'La ikraa fi uddin,'*'' she quoted

suddenly from the Qu'ran, and then with pointed deliberation, measuring her words, translated it. "'There is no compulsion in religion.' Did you quote that to your mullahs, when they complained about your girlfriend's bathing suit?"

"No, I did not," he said flatly. "And they did not co—"

"You did not. Let me guess. You sat there being embarrassed—embarrassed because there you were, a man wanting to rule a country, and you couldn't even keep your own woman in line. Is that about it?"

"No, that is not about it!"

"Well, good! Because leaving aside the fact that I am *not* your woman, why should you be keeping your woman in line, Ashraf? Why do men—"

But as if her words had unleashed some rage that he had been keeping in uneasy check, with two steps he was standing before her. His hands wrapped her upper arms.

"Not my woman? You are my woman!" he growled at her, and with no more warning than a gasp, she was in his arms, being painfully held, and fiercely kissed.

Her blood roared up in answer, fast, hot and filled with thunder. Her mouth opened to receive the hungry thrust of his tongue, her body pressed against the sudden hard searching of his.

One hand released her arm to encircle her naked waist under her open shirt, his hand hot against her spine. The other slid up to cup her neck. She was melting with the passion of wanting him. The suddenness of his cracking overwhelmed her.

His kiss was almost cruel with passionate hunger. He lifted his mouth only to cast a burning look into her eyes and then smother her lips again.

Dana almost wept with the relief of holding him and touching him after an age of yearning. Waves of delight so strong it was almost pain swept her. When he lifted his mouth at last, she pressed her lips against his strong, brown throat and planted little kisses from his chin to the neck of his kaftan. She felt him kiss her ear, her temple, felt his fingers thread her damp hair.

He was murmuring her name as if the sound intoxicated him. The passion in his arms, his body, his voice made her weak with desire. With trembling fingers he drew the shirt away from her shoulders, down her arms, let it fall to the floor. He pulled off his *keffiyeh* and she heard the shoosh of its landing by her feet.

For a moment his hands were tight on her waist, and then he turned and led her to the bed. She sank down onto it as Ashraf lifted his kaftan over his head and tossed it aside. He was naked underneath, and she watched his magnificent body for a moment of delight before he reached for the light switch. His hand moved and darkness descended around them.

The lamp on the dressing table cast a small double circle of soft light, itself and its reflection in the mirror. Then Ashraf came between her eyes and the glow, and pushed her down on the bed. And then there was nothing but shadow and delight.

Hours later she lay in the circle of his arms, purring with contentment, his hand gently stroking her skin. What a lover he was! She had never experienced anything so thorough as the pleasure he had given her.

"Do you feel guilty?" she asked.

There was a smile on his lips which she had longed to put there. "Guilty? No. I feel reluctant to leave you, as I soon will have to."

"More meetings tomorrow?"

He nodded. "I must prepare."

Suddenly the world came rushing back. "Is it the mullahs again?"

He moved his lips. "No. We'll meet for further talks when I get back to London."

"Are you going to cut a deal with them?"

His hand stroked her back. "Dana, the future of Bagestan depends upon my coming to some agreement with them."

She sat up, all the lazy honey he had set adrift in her system with his lovemaking drying up with a suddenness that shocked her.

"Bull," she said. She turned to look down at him in the shadows. "*Bull*, Ashraf! That is just not true. If you let those men help you to the throne, you've won the battle but lost the war. If they get a grip on you now, you will never be free of them." She reached for the light by the bed and flicked it on. She knelt on their love-tossed bed and bent over him.

"Look at the papers. The people of Bagestan are standing in the streets, more of them every day, tens of thousands of them by now. Silently, just watching. Waiting. What more do you need? How much of an invitation do they have to give you? What do they have to do to prove that they're behind you, and no mullah, no matter how popular, or how rabid, will sway them?"

"Of course they—"

But the passion of truth was urgent in her. "You don't need the oil companies, either, Ash. You don't need to sell out your reign to anyone. The people are your strength, and they won't be asking for concessions. All they want is to be free to live their lives as they judge right. And if that's not your first priority, what's the point of the whole exercise?"

"There is more to a coup than riding through the streets on a white horse," he told her, in bitter imitation of her own words. "If there is no stability afterwards, if the economy descends into chaos, where are we? I have to achieve stability before anything else can be achieved. If the *ulema* and the oil companies and other nations of the world are not behind me, tossing Ghasib out is no more than a gesture. That is why we play these games with the Western press. To make the world aware of the situation, so that informed public opinion is on our side.

"The people want freedom, you say. But they also want a functioning economy. Look at Russia. Do you think the people are happier there today than they were under Communism? The rouble drops every day. The economy is in the hands of gangsters. The people yearn for the stability of former times! And why? Because the country was left to drift after the overthrow. Because the West did not come to Russia's aid during the transition period. I do not want this to happen in Bagestan. Bad as Ghasib is, he nevertheless represents a certain stability. I cannot sacrifice that stability in the name of liberty."

"All right, you have to have them on your side! But that's afterwards," she said. "What is the point of dealing with these people—any of them—when you have no real authority yet and they know it? Of course they'll push you for the hardest possible deal when you're weak.

"You can get the authority of the people behind you first. You don't need the oil companies and the *ulema* and the multinationals to do it. You're looking at it backwards. What you need is the people behind you—to help you deal with the oil companies and the multinationals and the mullahs. Not the other way around.''

He lay thoughtfully watching her. ''This is fine as an ideal. But there are practicalities to consider, Dana.''

She sighed and shook her head, then got up and stood looking down at him. ''How much are you going to give way on women's rights?''

He watched how anguish shadowed her eyes even as the lamplight shadowed her beautiful body, and wished he did not have to answer. ''I have told you. As little as possible.''

She shook her head, turned away, and went to the bathroom. When she came back he was gone.

Their dinner *à deux* was strained. She seemed to have waited forever to have him to herself again, and now she was too hurt to enjoy it. She thought bitterly that he was right—they should not have made love while he was involved so deeply with this. But even as she thought it, her body melted with gratitude for his lovemaking and the need for more.

The food, as always, was delicious. They tried to talk about other things as they ate—about her television experiences, about Shakespeare, even about the Night of the Thousand and One Books. But there was always a tiny frown of preoccupation in his eyes, and of unhappiness in hers.

''You don't think William Shakespeare wrote the plays of Shakespeare?'' he repeated in surprise.

''I think the name *William Shake-speare* was a pseudonym,'' she said. ''And I think the man William Shakspere of Stratford on Avon was hired to front for someone who couldn't admit he was the playwright.''

''Who would that someone be?''

But though it was a favourite hobbyhorse of hers, she couldn't get excited by the subject tonight.

"Are you—devoted to your acting career?" Ashraf asked her a moment later.

She shrugged. "I don't even know. Sometimes I think I only went into acting because it was the thing my father would hate most. Even when I was a young teenager people were always saying I should be an actor or a model, but my father always said categorically that it was something I would never do, and I didn't mind much. Then when I was sixteen—well, that was when I suddenly saw how desperately in love with the theatre I was. And I auditioned for RADA and got in. And that was that."

He looked as though he could understand more than she was saying. "Why sixteen? This is the second time you have mentioned that age. What happened at sixteen, Dana, to turn your life upside down?"

She took a tiny bite of food and chewed it. Then she said quietly, "I learned that my father had stolen me from my mother and kept us apart for ten years. All the while she tore the world apart looking for me, and I cried myself to sleep at nights wishing she had loved me enough to stay with us. He told me she didn't. He didn't tell her anything at all. He just disappeared with me one day. For weeks she thought we must be dead in some accident. Then she discovered he had taken out a passport for me."

Ashraf gazed at her throughout the recital, deeply disturbed. "That's a tragic, desperate story," he said. "What grief must have been caused you both."

She felt the ready tears spring to her eyes, more easily because her emotions were so near the surface tonight.

"Yes," she said, her voice tight. "But he was happy,

so that made it all right. He got married again, and had another daughter, to a Muslim woman who didn't put her daughter's soul in danger with tales of Coyote and Bear and Gitchi Manitou. He was protecting me, of course," she pointed out with dry sarcasm. "He wasn't thinking selfishly at all. He had to save me from my mother and her paganism."

He seemed to have no reply for this. They sat and ate in silence for a while.

"And how did you find your mother? Did your father tell you at last?" he asked.

"Oh, no! I don't think he would ever have done that. My mother tracked me down. She'd spent most of the ten years trying to get information in Bagestan and Barakat, because my father had left a false trail. I don't know what clue suddenly made her start to look in England." She paused. "I swore not to speak to my father for ten years, so that he could taste a little of her experience."

Ashraf looked shocked. "And you—you kept your oath?"

She nodded. "But not for the full ten years. I was at boarding school, and then drama school, and I spent all my holidays with my mother for five or six years and hardly saw him. After that I relaxed a bit. I never visited him, but if he came to see me I didn't throw him out, either. Sometimes he came to the theatre when I was in a show. He must have hated that."

Ashraf said, "Your father had suffered much. It is no surprise if grief and stress made him a little mad. Have you not been able to take the past into account and forgive him? Even now?"

"What past? Bagestan suffered a coup, and in common with many other Bagestanis, he fled and started his life again in Canada.''

''But your father had a wife, a son and daughter in Bagestan. They were killed by Ghasib's murder squad. You do not consider this grounds for special grief?''

Dana set down her fork and stared at him. ''What? Who told you this?''

''You do not know it?''

''I've never heard a word of it!''

He twisted his head. ''It is true, nonetheless.''

''How can it be? And how do you happen to know?''

''All my family knows the history of Colonel Loghatullah. It was taught to us in our cradles, so that we should never forget the service he performed or the debt we owe.''

''My father's name is Golbahn,'' she pointed out, with a curious look.

''That is the name he took when he escaped to the West. In Parvani, it means, *Protector of the Rose*. Are you really aware of none of this?''

She was staring at him in a mixture of astonishment and horror. ''No one has ever said a word to me about...'' Dana faded off, as vague memories surfaced. The Bagestanis who were always in and out of their flat, smiling at her with damp eyes, and saying things like, *You have a very brave, wonderful father*.

She remembered something else, too.

''Is *this* why you tried to give me a cheque that day?''

He lifted his hands in acknowledgement.

''What service did he perform for your family?'' she demanded.

Ashraf looked curiously at her. ''But you are half Bagestani. Does the name Colonel Loghatullah mean nothing to you?''

She shook her head emphatically. "The only Colonel Loghatullah I ever heard of all my life long is the courageous Colonel Loghatullah who led the Palace Guard resistance and saved the lives of the royal...oh, my *God!*" She dropped her fork and clapped her hands over her mouth.

"Are you—Ashraf, are you telling me that...that my father...?"

Ashraf smiled gently. "Is the great hero of the Bagestani coup. Yes. The man who carried the Crown Princess and her son to safety in Parvan, and for payment saw his own wife and children murdered. The man without whom my entire family would have been slaughtered on the first day of the coup.

"I would not be sitting here with you today, were it not for your father, Dana. I would never have been born were it not for his great courage, and his sacrifice."

Thirteen

———

The candles on the table seemed to darken. Dana rested her head in her hand as nausea gripped her. Hot tears sprang to her eyes and spilled down her cheeks.

"My father—*Allah,* is it possible? Why didn't he *tell* me?"

"Perhaps he felt that you were too young to keep the secret. He, too, was in danger from Ghasib's hit squads. And when you were older…"

When she was older he had had no opportunity. She sniffed and wiped her eyes with her fingers, staring at him. "You've just explained so much in my life!" she told him. "Oh, God, his utter obsession with the restoration—he made me obsessed, too. I told you I used to write letters to the Crown Prince! And then—oh!" She sighed. She squeezed her eyes shut, wiped tears from her cheeks again. "All those people, always coming and talking about the good old days...oh, it all makes sense!''

She sat back in her chair, propping her chin in her hand, as the tears burned their way down her cheeks. She looked at Ashraf again. ''His wife and children were killed?''

''It was Ghasib's revenge. When your father led Princess Hana and the infant Prince Kamil to safety in Parvan, word followed him of what had happened. He never went back.''

Of course she had heard the story, in the past. But then it had been the story of a distant hero, not her own father's life.

It was long before she could feel she had absorbed it, and she knew that it would be a lot longer than tonight before all the repercussions had settled in her psyche. They finished dinner, still talking it over, and took their coffee cups to the loungers.

At length, he said, ''Dana, do you understand a little better my anger this afternoon? The mullahs were informed that the daughter of Colonel Loghatullah would be on the yacht. I was hoping to introduce you to them. I had told them...''

He broke off, as if thinking better of what he had been going to say.

She turned curiously. ''What?''

There was a silence as he considered his course of action. Then he said quietly, ''I told them that I hoped to marry you. They—they drew from this the inference that we were already engaged. I didn't correct that misapprehension.''

She stared at him, her heart beating hard. ''Marry! What—why did you tell them that?''

''Because it is true. I want to marry you, Dana.''

She opened her mouth for air. Her heart was full to bursting; there was too much feeling for her to hold it all. "But you're...Ash!" she exploded disbelievingly. "You're going to be the Sultan of Bagestan!"

"Yes. It will be a great endeavour," he said simply. "And I ask you to be my partner in this endeavour, Dana."

Her heart was melting with love and need. She smiled and pressed her lips together, then bit her lower lip and looked at the stars, trying not to cry again. "Ash—" she began, knowing suddenly that there was nothing she wanted more than to be his wife. But—

"Ash, that would mean living in Bagestan."

"Would it be so terrible a fate?" he asked, with a suppressed anguish in his tone, as if he feared what her answer would be.

She stood up, went and leaned over the railing to look into the darkness and the stars. Her world was completely unrecognizable from what it had been two weeks ago. Everything was changed. She groped for a rudder in the stormy sea of her life.

He let her stand there for several minutes, then got up to stand beside her. She looked out at the sea. It looked so tranquil, but then, so did this moment. And under the surface all kinds of things were stirring and in turmoil.

"Ash, you're going to meet with the mullahs in a few days in order to barter with women's rights. You're asking me to be a wife in a *hejab*," she said.

"Dana—"

"A second-class citizen, whose rights are to be dictated by the whim of a lot of old men using God for their own ends."

"It may not come to that," he said urgently. "I may—"

"You may be able to convince them to go easy on women?" She shook her head. "Ash, don't you see that you've already given in? Just the idea that you *may* convince them—you've given them the power. What right have you got—no, but I've said it all."

She heaved a deep, trembling sigh. "No, Ash. No. If you want a lover for those times when the Sultan of Bagestan visits the West, I'm your woman. But don't ask me to go and be the sultana of a country where my sex has been sold down the river. I won't do it."

He was turning her to him, drawing her into his hold with ruthless passion. "What are you saying? I want a wife, not a lover when I am in the West!" he cried angrily. "Why do you taunt me like this? I looked on you and loved you, don't you understand? You are the only woman I will ever want! Please. Whatever arrangement we come to with the *ulema,* it will not be onerous, Dana. It will sit lightly on most women, I promise. I will not agree to anything very restrictive."

She looked at him. "I was born free," she said simply.

"You could use your talents and experience in Bagestan. There is much to be done revitalizing the old culture, the arts—you could make a great contribution, Dana."

She was shaken, but she knew she was right. She couldn't live like that. It would drive her crazy. "If your bid fails, Ashraf, I'll marry you like a shot. As long as you agree to live in the West. I couldn't say no. But until and unless women in Bagestan have the same civil, social and economic rights as men—I won't cross the border. Think what you're asking, Ash, and then ask yourself if it's love to ask that sacrifice of me."

* * *

"Hi, Roxy."

"Dana? Are you back in London?"

"Yes. I'm still—"

"Oh, they told me he was coming back today, and that you'd be with him!" Roxy exclaimed.

"Did they? Who?"

"Khalid Abd al Darogh. He said he wants to see you as soon as possible."

"Does he," Dana said flatly. "I wonder why he thinks he can dictate to me like that?"

"Dana, you have to go! Please—I'm scared. He's—last time he said something about Daddy. I didn't understand it, but it sounded like some kind of threat to hurt him."

"And you want me to go and face him, huh? What gets me, Roxy, is the surprise in your voice, as if you had no idea people could be so nasty. But Dad told you all about these men last time you got into trouble, didn't he? So I'm wondering why you are so amazed to come up against it now."

She was being hard, but her softness in the past, she could see now, had done her sister no favours. If Roxy had the feeling that there were no consequences to her actions, who had assisted her to come to that conclusion?

"You don't always believe everything Daddy says!" Roxy exploded.

"Right. So the position is, they're threatening to do some physical violence against Dad, so you want me to go and see them instead," Dana said dryly.

"No!—well, yes, but…look, Dana, I've been thinking. Don't you think it would be easier to just ask Sheikh Ashraf for the money to pay them off? I mean, if he's really a sultan, he must be loaded."

"And why would he give me such a huge amount of money?" Dana had to scotch this, because Ashraf and his team wanted to learn what the casino owners planned.

"Well, you...I mean, after all—"

"I'm sorry, I'm not in a position to ask the sheikh to pay my sister's gambling debts."

"No, but I thought—couldn't you pretend they were your own?"

She drew a long, deep breath. "No," Dana said flatly. "Not to them, and not to you."

"You see," Roxy said sulkily, "when I do try to protect you, you won't listen."

Dana laughed with real amusement. "That's how you see it, is it? Well, I'm sorry to reject your deep consideration for my continued good health, Roxy. However, I will meet with them and find out what they want. So suppose you arrange that?"

Ashraf was sitting in the main room of their hotel suite with Naj, Harry and several advisors—two of whom, she noted with surprise, were women. They all looked up as she entered, but it was Ash's gaze she returned. He put out his hand and she came around to the empty chair next to him.

"Any trouble?" he asked.

"No, they didn't threaten me or anything, or even ask to search me." Which was just as well, because she had been miked up to the bodyguards Ashraf had had tailing her.

Everyone was silent, waiting. She heaved a breath. "They want me to insist on taking that prize dinner at the Riverfront you bid £15,000 for. I'm supposed to book a table in the conservatory. Someone is going to walk up and say your name, and then hand you a sub-poena. I should just play ignorant.''

Everyone exchanged glances. There was no need to repeat the obvious—that it was going to be an assassination attempt, not a newspaper exposé, not an accusation of brutality.

''When?'' Ash asked.

''Five days from now,'' she said.

A helicopter took them to a beautiful estate on the coast of Cornwall belonging to Sir John Cross, the former ambassador to Bagestan and Parvan, who had sat beside her at the Drought Relief fund-raiser.

There the meetings began again.

Sometimes, when they were alone, they fought. He wanted her to say she would marry him, to trust him to deal with the *ulema*'s demands in a reasonable way. She tried to make him understand why she could not.

''What *good* does it do them, anyway, to force women to obey a religious diktat, even if it was prescribed in the Qu'ran?'' she demanded once.

''What do you mean?''

''It's not going to improve *my* soul, or my relationship with God, if I only obey the rules because I'm forced to! And it's not going to do their souls any good, because nowhere does it say you get a reward for forcing someone else to be good! So what's the point, from a religious perspective?''

''You are asking me to get inside the mind of a religious leader. I do not know the answer to this.''

''There's no law anywhere forcing people to fast during Ramadan, is there?'' Dana went on wildly. ''Why not?''

''I don't—''

"You know why not! Because religion is meant to be a matter of conscience! But somehow, that fact gets lost when it comes to a question of women's duties!"

"Why do you put these arguments to me, when you know that I agree with you? I am faced with a political problem—how to take over with the least possible disruption in the country. To do this, I have explained to you—"

"You have to compromise! Well, that's your choice made, then, Ashraf! And that's fine. But don't expect *me* to agree to the selling of my rights and freedom just because you choose to do it. You are making a choice for your life that includes being Sultan of Bagestan, but excludes having me as your wife. That's it."

Always they parted with bitterness.

He would not make love to her. When she tried to soothe her hurt in his arms, he held her, but would not give in to her passionate longing.

"I want a wife, not a lover," he told her again. "If I have to live without you, Dana, what good will it do me to have fed my need of you with lovemaking? You are already in my blood. Do you think I am not tortured by the desire to leave the country to its fate? To say to my brother, let it be you who rules? To have you and damn the world?

"I cannot do it. My duty has been marked out for me since the moment of my cousin Kamil's death. But even before that, I knew that my life would be circumscribed by the family's duty to Bagestan. You force a choice on me that gives me unending torment. Well, I must live with that. But I will not voluntarily increase my pain by learning all the ways of your body and my own pleasure, knowing all the while that it is not to be mine."

She was weeping when he finished.

Dana wandered the estate during the hot August days, trying to see some way out of her dilemma. She loved him, she wanted to marry him. But he was destined to be the Sultan of Bagestan. He could not give that up for her sake, but nor could she make the sacrifice of her rights, however desperately her love tore at her heart and pleaded with her that no sacrifice was too great when such love as this was at stake.

They had separate bedrooms. She was always awake when he came upstairs at night, after a late meeting, and she always waited and hoped for the sound of his footsteps to pause outside her door. But he never came to her. And she would not go to him.

"Good afternoon, ladies and gentlemen. Thank you for coming today," said Ashraf Durran ibn Wafiq ibn Hafzuddin al Jawadi.

The lawn was crammed with reporters. A helicopter seemed to have arrived every five minutes for the past two hours to disgorge more. In front of the house the cars were lined up for a mile down both sides of the pretty, narrow lane.

Bleachers of a sort had been arranged on the lawn, providing three levels, so that those at the back would not have their view blocked. Dana hadn't seen so many television cameras in one place except in movies.

Ashraf, with Harry, Najib and Gazi al Hamzeh around him, was standing on the terrace in front of a microphone stand. There were so many microphones it looked like a bunch of giant grapes.

"I think—" Ashraf smiled a little ruefully at the crowd out on the lawn "—that some of you may have guessed what I am here to say."

A murmur of appreciation rippled through his audience.

"So let me say it." He lifted his right hand. "This ring is the al Jawadi Rose. It has been passed from the reigning monarch to his nominated heir in Bagestan for many, many generations. Even in my family, no one knows who was the first monarch to wear the Rose."

The clicking and whirring of cameras was almost deafening as photographers angled to get a shot of Prince Ashraf with his hand lifted, and do justice to the magnificent pink diamond that glowed on his forefinger.

"My grandfather was Sultan Hafzuddin al Jawadi. This ring tells you that I am my grandfather's nominated heir for the throne of Bagestan. And I call on President Ghasib to heed the will of the people, which is being expressed daily in the streets of Medinat al Bostan and throughout Bagestan. I call upon President Ghasib to resign his ill-gotten place, and leave the country for wherever he may find a safe haven. I ask him to do this immediately and peacefully. And I expect to take back the throne of my family within the next few days."

It was no more than they had come for, but Ashraf's charisma added an unexpected element to the equation. There was excitement in the air, and not just because they knew they had a story that was going to give them front page copy for days, if not weeks.

"I know that there are representatives here from the media in Bagestan. I ask them to take this message back to the people of Bagestan," Ash continued. He turned his head and looked straight into two cameras which had been put in a privileged position just to one side, and began to speak in Bagestani Arabic.

With all her listening practice lately, Dana could just about follow his speech. "...I know that you have suffered much under the cruel hand that has had you in its grip for the past thirty years and more. The sight of your sufferings was a grief to my honoured grandfather and to my father after him, and it continues a grief to me.

"But if you wish it, your suffering is at an end. If you desire it, I will restore the throne of the al Jawadi, who have ruled you in good times and bad, but always with your happiness at heart...."

"His Excellency will take a few questions if you wish." Gazi stepped to the mike when Ashraf had finished; Gazi was the stage manager of the press conference.

A hundred hands snapped into the air. Gazi pointed first to a reporter from Bagestan. The question was asked and answered in Arabic.

Gazi's management of the conference was virtually flawless. There were reporters from all around the world in attendance, and he was managing to take one question from each of two dozen different nations. And although the majority of the questions were put in English, Ashraf also answered with fair fluency those that were asked in French and Parvani, and even managed a brief response in Japanese, which everyone applauded.

He answered with an intelligence and a grasp of world affairs that clearly impressed everyone, jaded as they might be. His personality and charisma came over amazingly, Dana saw. They might have come expecting someone very different, but they quickly grasped the fact that Ashraf was no fool.

"What is the import of the title His Excellency?" someone called at the end. "Is that the traditional address for the sultan?"

"It is the address used to the Cup Companions of the Barakat Emirates, a position His Excellency still holds.

He will not use the titles reserved for the Sultan of Bagestan until he is actually on the throne.''

That was the last question. Ashraf bowed and turned back inside, while the assembled burst into applause.

"Stage One complete," said Gazi.

Fourteen

————

"**I**'m going to outline the overall arrangements now for everyone," Naj said. "Each of you has had a particular briefing already."

The room, the sitting room of a huge suite at the top of one of London's most famous and expensive hotels, was filled with men and women, all listening attentively.

"As most of you know, we'll have a very strong presence in the Riverfront Restaurant tonight. Some of you are going to be busboys, some patrons. Just under half the tables are full, including our agents and the ordinary patrons of the place.

"You've all been given individual schedules that tell you when to arrive. Ash's booking is for nine o'clock, and most of you will be in position by that time....

"Ash will sit in the conservatory. Three of you dressed in similar clothes will also be seated there.

Amina's standing in for Dana—she'll keep her headscarf over her face as far as she can.''

Dana had argued and argued for the right to go as herself. Some inner conviction told her she should be there. But Ashraf and the others had rejected the idea completely. She was to stay safe in the hotel till it was all over. She had barely managed to convince Ash to let her come up to London to help with her stand-in's disguise.

''They warned me I'd have to wear platforms to get the extra height,'' Amina complained to her a short time later, in the dressing room that led off Dana's bedroom. Dana was helping the agent to dress in some of her own clothes. Amina had stripped to her underwear and was walking around in a pair of platform heels, getting used to them. ''They don't really let you connect to the ground, do they?''

Dana only shook her head. ''I've never worn platforms.''

Amina looked at her and laughed. ''Well, at five-eleven I guess you wouldn't. Where's that vest?''

Dana lifted the bulletproof vest and held it up for her. It was heavy, but not as bulky as she'd imagined. Amina slipped her arms in, pulled the flap between her legs and up over her abdomen, pressed all the fasteners.

Dana next held up a pair of *shalwar* in a black silk-linen mix, then the embroidered black tunic. It was an outfit she had chosen to Najib's instructions—the pants were drawstring, and the *kamees* was full, to disguise the thickness of the protective vest. The outfit was completed with a black-and-silver scarf which she helped the agent pin securely in her long, dark hair—the only thing in which she really resembled Dana—and draped it around her lower face.

"Right!" said Amina, consulting her watch. "Zero hour. Wish me luck."

"Good luck," Dana said with a smile, moving backwards out of the dressing room. She drew the door closed behind her, and turned the key to lock it. "Sorry," she called through the panels, as Amina gave a cry of surprise. "But you understand, I have to be there."

She had purchased a brand of perfume she had never worn before, and moving quickly now she sprayed it liberally on her hair and skin. Then from the bed she picked up the peach scarf that matched her own silky outfit, and sprayed that before wrapping it carefully around her face and head.

As she left the room she could hear Amina start to pound the door, but the hotel was one of the old, solidly built kind, and when she closed the bedroom door the sound died.

One of the bodyguards was waiting for her in the hall.

"Come," he said. "We are two minutes behind time. The others have gone down."

This was a piece of luck! Dana relaxed and knew suddenly that it was going to work. She had been most worried about Ash recognizing her in the elevator.

Three limousines were waiting in the hotel drive. Ash, wearing a flowing white djellaba and luxurious *keffiyeh* with gold ropes, was standing at one side talking to Harry. Dana went past without looking towards him, hiding her hands under her scarf as she held it over her face.

Suddenly she was almost laughing. Only a few days ago she had told him she would never put on *hejab* for his sake, and here she was, as terrified of showing her face as the most downtrodden of women!

The door of the second limo was opened for her and Dana slipped inside and drew back into the corner. The bodyguard followed, and sat facing her on the pull-down seat. A moment later Ash and another bodyguard got in and the first limousine moved out into the street. Their own followed, and behind them came the third.

They sat mostly silent in the darkness, each of them thinking about the task ahead. Dana said nothing at all, just kept as far from Ash as she could. Fortunately the limousine had a pull-down arm between their seats.

Her heart was pumping hard, but didn't really start to thunder until they pulled up at the Riverfront Restaurant. There, wrapping her scarf very securely around her face, as Amina would have done, Dana followed the body-guard out of the car.

The bodyguard led the way down the gangplank into the restaurant, Dana following, then Ashraf, then the second bodyguard. It seemed little enough protection, but she reminded herself that the restaurant itself was filled with agents, and probably so was the street.

"Good evening, Miss Morningstar, good evening, Your Excellency. What a great pleasure." The maître d' smiled a welcome as Ashraf stopped just behind her. She felt Ash's firm grip on her upper arm.

"What the hell do you think you're doing?" he hissed in her ear. She turned and smiled at him, and saw by the shock on his face that he could hardly believe his eyes.

She turned to follow after the maître d', and Ash had to let her go. He could not create a scene for fear of triggering some reaction in the agents.

"It's Reena!" she heard the whispers as she moved past various tables, and she felt the strangeness of being in that old world suddenly, when all her concentration was in the new one.

The front deck of the old ship had been enclosed with a large bubble of glass, giving a beautiful view of the Thames. The massive Ferris wheel called the London Eye dominated the skyline on the other side of the river.

"What the devil are you doing here?" he demanded in an undervoice when they were seated at a table alone, the two bodyguards ostentatiously placed at a table nearby. That was to convince anyone watching that these two were all there were.

"You know this would all be jeopardized without me," Dana returned, unapologetically, talking into her menu. "Why did you try to prevent me?"

"Order a meal, and then get up and go to the ladies' room and stay there," he ordered her furiously.

"Don't let the headscarf fool you," Dana said sweetly. "It hasn't changed anything. I'm still a free woman. And I make my own choices."

The drinks waiter arrived with a bottle of the best champagne in the house. It was all part of the prize for which Ashraf had paid fifteen thousand pounds. Ash let him pop the cork and pour the champagne, watched as the attentive waiter set the bottle in an ice bucket beside the table. Then he quietly ordered water in addition.

Dana had no intention of drinking alcohol tonight, but she picked up her glass nevertheless. "Pick it up and toast me," she said. "Otherwise we are going to look all wrong."

Furious as he was, he knew she was right. He picked up his glass and saluted her, then replaced it on the table without making any pretence of drinking. Dana smiled and pretended to sip, but she didn't taste a drop. Tonight was the night for a completely clear head.

Another waiter was coming towards them, with a small tray and two glasses on it. Dana blinked and felt a buzz of alarm. There was some anomaly which her subconscious mind had picked up, but she couldn't get consciously. She stared at him.

"Ash," she said warningly, and then it clicked—there was no bottle of water on the tray....and she had seen the man before. In Fuad al Kadthib's office at the casino, the second time she had met him.

Ash reacted instantly to the change in her tone. He lifted his arm and looked at his watch in the prearranged signal of trouble.

The waiter came towards the table, a tray clasped in one hand, balanced over the other. And for Dana the world suddenly went into slow motion. She saw the man lift the tray slightly, saw the dull glint of metal under it. Watched her own hand go out to the ice bucket and wrap the neck of the champagne bottle.

Ash, meanwhile, put both hands on the edge of the table and shoved.

The champagne bottle, spilling its foamy contents in a wide arc, smashed down on the metal tray with a whang to wake the world, just as the table smacked into the man's groin. He made a strangled sound.

For Dana time returned to normal.

Someone shouted. The gun exploded three times in quick succession, a nasty little *pfutt! pfutt! pfutt!* as the assassin staggered back. The first hit the table, the second hit Ash, the third hit the glass of the conservatory behind his head.

"*Ash!*" Dana screamed. His chair went over backwards under the blow, and as he went down on the floor she flung herself out of her own chair and across his head and body in instinctive protection. "Ash! Ash!"

Over her head there was uproar as agents erupted from half the tables in the room and converged on the man with the gun. Men and women screamed and shouted, some falling to the floor, others frozen in their seats, still others running this way or that.

Then suddenly there was stillness.

"Ash!" Dana sobbed again, scrabbling to her knees to look down at him. He was lying with his face contorted, his hand clutching his ribs. "Oh, God, Ash, are you hit?"

He opened his eyes and grinned at her. "Yes, I'm hit," he said. "*Allah,* a bullet packs a wallop, even when you're wearing body armour!"

The first rays of the summer morning were coming up over the green hills as the helicopter rose away from the lawn and the peace of the Cornish countryside enveloped them. The butler let them into the otherwise still sleeping house and, Ash's arm around Dana's waist, they went upstairs.

Her bedroom door was reached first, but Ash simply ignored it, drawing Dana past it and along to his own room. Her heart kicked with reaction, and she looked a smile up at him. The expression she saw in his eyes melted her.

It was a beautiful room, with wide windows open onto the green lawn and the forest, and a large antique four-poster bed. The oak floor glowed with the polish of centuries under Bagestani and Parvani rugs spread as if at random.

They walked over to one of the windows beside the bed and stood looking out for a moment. A deer stood in the protection of the trees at the edge of the lawn, flicking her ears, watching. They waited in silence, let-

ting the peace sink into their bones, as the beautiful crea-
ture at last stepped out onto the lush grass and, with
another flick of her delicate ears, bent to eat.

He turned to her and lifted one strong hand to her
cheek and temple, looking into her face, and thinking
how like the deer she was—elegant, graceful, beautiful,
but quick and strong. The eyes she watched him with
were like the deer's, too. Wide, dark, and slanting, and
full of a mystery that had captured him with that first,
challenging glance.

She laid her hands flat against his chest and tilted her
head for his kiss, and he realized that he could never
have resisted her. His mouth took the offering with a
hunger and a passion that made them both moan. Then
he held her head in his hands and kissed her cheek, her
ear, and down the long graceful line of her neck.

After endless, tenderly passionate kisses, he led her to
the bed and slowly slipped the pale silk of her clothes
from her body, till was standing in only a tiny pair
of briefs. He caressed the long line of her naked back
while she busied herself unbuttoning his shirt.

She gasped when she pulled it open, for the place
where the bullet had slammed into him was now marked
with a huge, black bruise. Just under his heart.

She bent and kissed it with feather kisses, murmuring
her concern.

Ashraf laughed and drew her face back up to his.
"That is not the worst wound I have had in my life,"
he told her. "Not by any means."

She bit her lip. "Really?"

"I was hit with a fatal shot the first time you looked
at me. And I was wearing no protective armour then. It
went straight to my heart." She gasped. "It is still there,
in my heart. You will be always there."

Dana smilingly shook her head. "The first time I looked at you," she accused him, "you were looking daggers at me! I've never seen such disapproval."

He touched her cheek. "I was angry with you then. You came into the room, and it was as if you brought beauty and nobility with you. There was a glow around you. I know you are a famous actress, but I had never seen you. I didn't know anything about you, except that I was destined to win you and you were destined to be mine.

"And then—you turned, and your dress became transparent. At first I thought you could not know, but I soon saw by your face that you did. I was so angry with you!" He smiled and drew the warmth of his hands down her back, around and up her abdomen and stomach until his hands rested just under the swell of her breasts. "I thought, she is mine, how does she show the world what is mine?"

Dana's heart melted, even as she shook her head. "Oh, Ashraf!"

"That was when you looked at me. And your look said—*I do not accept your judgement of what I do!*"

A little burst of laughter escaped her because of the truth of it.

"And then I knew that I would make you mine, but that the road to your love would not be an easy one for me. And I was right."

They lay on the bed then, naked and entranced with each other's body. His hands were perfect on her skin. There had never been a touch that thrilled her so. He made her melt and freeze and melt again, till she could do no more than whimper his name.

Then he rose up over her, slipped his legs between her helplessly spread thighs, and pushed into the connection they both needed. They cried out together, and smiled, already tasting the joy to come, and knew that this was what their souls had yearned for.

"Dana, I love you," he said later, as they lay in each other's arms in the wide bed. "Tell me you love me."

"I love you, Ash, oh, I love you!" she cried. "But please don't ask—"

He put his fingers to her lips and stilled her anguish. "Shh!" he commanded. "Have no more fears. I understand you, Dana. I did not see it so clearly before. You are a woman as brave as Nusaybah. And—"

"Nusaybah?"

"She was a warrior. Before the Battle of Uhud she asked the Prophet's permission to bear arms as a warrior. He gave her that permission. And when the day went against him, and the enemy broke through, Nusaybah was among those who circled him, and stood between the Prophet and death. His life was saved."

Dana propped herself up on one arm and looked down at him with a surprised smile. "I've never heard that before!"

"It is recorded in certain biographies. I do not know why it is not more known. It is a clear lesson."

Dana sighed, and happiness seemed to flow through her. "Is it?"

"The Prophet allowed Nusaybah to follow the dictates of her own heart. If he had not done so, who can say whether he would have survived the disaster of Uhud? Why should ordinary men do otherwise? Are we so much wiser than the Prophet that we can instruct women in their religion?"

She was silent, but her heart was full to bursting.

"You saved my life last night, Dana."

"Mash'Allah," she murmured. *It was God's will.* And that was no more than the truth. She had not acted entirely from herself. She had been inspired.

"I was a fool to gainsay your determination to go to the restaurant with me. But I am not a Prophet, and wisdom comes slowly to men. I am grateful that you refused to substitute my judgement for your own, and I hope I will never again ask such a thing of you. And I see that you are right in what you said. I cannot allow myself to rule over a nation where any woman's conscience is dictated by the law.

"On those terms, Dana, I ask you to marry me. To be my wife and my sultana. To be the mother of my children, and to govern my people beside me."

She was weeping too hard to answer.

"Assalaamu aleikum," Ashraf said, as the bearded, turbaned men clambered out of the helicopter, their robes flapping in the wind that the slowly beating rotors stirred up.

"Waleikum assalaam."

They exchanged formal greetings and bows, and he led them across the green lawn towards the sprawling manor house.

He stopped a few yards short of the door, and stretched out one arm to the left. Obediently they turned their eyes in the direction he pointed. There was nothing to see but the shrubbery surrounding the lawn. But before they could ask, he turned and led them inside the house and along a wide hall.

Again, Prince Ashraf stopped and pointed, this time towards the end of the hall. Again their eyes followed the direction of his finger. An antique oak dresser with a small inlaid mirror and a potted plant. Above it, something framed. Nothing of note, and the men wondered and exchanged mystified glances.

Inside the formal dining room, equipped now as a boardroom, they quickly dispersed to the chairs allotted to them. Prince Ashraf's team, men and women, were interspersed among the mullahs, rather than on the opposite side of the table, as a way of reducing confrontation. Ashraf went to the head of the table, where he remained on his feet.

When they were all settled and looking his way, he pointed again, at a corner of the ceiling. Murmuring with confusion now, the men nevertheless could not resist looking in the direction indicated by his clenched fist, his strong finger. There was nothing there.

When they looked back at him in bewilderment, he was holding a Qu'ran in his hand. "What is it you wish us to look at, Prince Ashraf?" one of the religious men asked.

"At my hand, of course," he said. He held it up.

"Your hand!"

"But you were pointing at something!"

"What?" he asked.

Now there were murmurs of disquiet and confusion. "You have been pointing as if to show us something."

Ashraf stared. "Do you mean that if I hold up my hand and point, you look not at my hand but in the direction to which I am pointing my finger?"

"But of course!" a bearded one cried, impatient. "This is true everywhere. A man points at what he wishes to draw one's attention to!"

Prince Ashraf looked around them in bewilderment. "Do you all agree with this idea?"

They were confused, disturbed, even angry. "Certainly," they muttered. "What else?"

"Each of you says the same thing?"

"Of course! Everyone knows it!"

Prince Ashraf smiled and lifted up the book in his hand. "Wise sirs," he said softly, "this Holy Qu'ran is the pointing finger of Allah. You all agree on the meaning of a pointing finger. Yet your focus is entirely fixed upon the book, and not on the direction in which it points."

They sat in astonished, bewildered silence, looking at Prince Ashraf, and at one another.

"If Allah allows men to act in a certain way, not because that way is right, but because He knows too well that mankind is weak, is it right for the faithful to carry on acting in that way, once they have discovered, through their own God-given wits, that it is wrong?"

They were speechless.

"If Mohammad, peace and blessings upon him, tells us that the greater jihad is not the battle against the infidel, but the battle to subdue the self, is it right for the faithful to neglect any aspect of the self which needs to be subdued?

"Today I give you notice that as Sultan of Bagestan I will ask you to turn your gaze in the direction to which the Holy Qu'ran points us. There are many hints within it that Allah expected us to travel further along the road that He had pointed out to us, rather than remaining exactly where He found us in the days of the Prophet.

"I say to you that it is no longer appropriate for men to consider the latitude Allah allowed to the ignorant and unruly men of earlier times as our guide. I will ask you for a new interpretation of Islamic law. In particular, as that law pertains to man's treatment of woman, to marriage, and to women's rights. But also in many other areas.

''I will ask you to consider the fact that the only instructions as to dress in the Holy Qu'ran are those given to the wives of the Prophet, and that until all men behave with the perfection of the Prophet, it is inappropriate to force all women to emulate the perfection of the Prophet's wives.

''These and many other considerations will be on the agenda.

''I say to you that the Door of *Ijtihad* must be opened again, and a fresh understanding of God's word discovered, which is appropriate for our own times.''

He paused and looked into their amazed, chagrined, curious faces. ''I tell you now so that you may be prepared for such discussions on the day when, *insha'Allah!* I become sultan in Bagestan.''

Fifteen

"**M**assive demonstrations have been taking place to-night in Medinat al Bostan, the capital of Bagestan. President Ghasib is reported to have fled. And Crown Prince Ashraf al Jawadi is said to be on his way to the country, where he expects to take command. With that story and more, here's Michael Druid."

"Good evening. Hundreds of thousands of people are massing around the walls of the New Palace in Medinat al Bostan tonight, as reports of the attempted assassination of Crown Prince Ashraf al Jawadi, which took place in London last night, reached the streets of Bagestan early today. We have no pictures yet, but John Sarwah is there, and he's on the line live from Bostan's Freedom Square. Hello, John."

"Hello, Michael. Well, there has never been anything like this, Michael, this is one of the most exciting moments of history I've witnessed. I'm in Freedom Square at the moment, opposite the main gate of the compound. The people are massed in absolutely unbelievable numbers all around the perimeter wall of the New Palace, filling not only the square, which is a massive space, but also all the streets leading to it, on all sides.

"Is it a silent vigil, John?"

"They're no longer silent. You can probably hear them in the background. They're screaming, they're chanting, they're demanding Ghasib's resignation. And they're also singing the underground song *Aina al Warda?* 'Where is the Rose?' That's been the song of the anti-Ghasibists, or rather the pro-Jawadi-ists, for a couple of decades now, but you'd better believe it hasn't been sung in public in Bagestan before."

"What sort of police presence is there?"

"None at all. That's one of the most remarkable things about it. There has been no police or military presence whatsoever, and since Ghasib has always had such close ties with the military, that fact alone tells the story."

"What's the mood of the crowd, John?"

"I would say angry and determined. They're battering the gates with logs and driving at them with a bus, and it's only a matter of minutes before those impregnable gates go down. But there's no mob hysteria."

"We've heard here that President Ghasib may no longer even be in the New Palace. What do you know about that?"

"Yes, that's the rumour circulating here, too. He may have already fled the country. People are also saying that Ashraf al Jawadi—well, there go the gates, John, can you hear the cheer going up around me? They are smashing through the gates, and the crowd is streaming into the compound. And there's not a sign of a guard, no shot has been fired in defence. There won't be much left of the noble New Palace by morning.

"I think that whatever happens now, John, we can say that this moment marked the end of President Ghasib's power in Bagestan."

"Well, Marta, it's a great day for Bagestan."

"Yes, Barry, thrilling times lately for the people of Bagestan, and just to recap—it's only six weeks since they stormed the New Palace to bring down the dictator Ghasib, and welcomed their new sultan's arrival, but that six weeks has brought tremendous change already, and today produces maybe the most exciting change of all.

"Will any of us ever forget the sight of the massive crowds who welcomed Sultan Ashraf al Jawadi as he rode *on horseback* through the streets of Medinat al Bostan to the Old Palace? The same crowds who stood in silent vigil for so many days in protest against Ghasib— who would have thought they would be cheering so loudly, and dancing in the streets, in so short a time? Here's some library film of those wild hours when a sultan came home again."

"We loof heem! We loof our sultaan!" a dark, heavy-set man screamed into a microphone, waving a banner, his eyes streaming with tears. He grabbed the Western reporter who stood beside him smiling bemusedly, and exuberantly kissed him. The camera drew back to show a long chain of dancing men and women, their arms twined around each other's shoulders, kicking their legs to the music of the song *Aina al Warda?*

"Djes! Djes!" a woman cried. "He brink us freedom, and good happiness, and we wont heem very much, for lonk time! And now he come!"

An aerial shot showed two thick ribbons of crowd,

lining either side of a boulevard that stretched for miles through the city, and then cut to the sight of handsome Sultan Ashraf al Jawadi, on a spirited white horse, riding slowly among the delirious crowds, accompanied by a dozen men also on horseback. He lifted his right hand at intervals, to show them the al Jawadi Rose on his finger. The cheers were deafening.

"It did the heart good, didn't it, Marta?" said Barry, as the camera returned to the studio.

"Yes, oh, it did," said Marta, wiping a corner of her eye. "It still makes me cry, even though I suppose that white horse was a bit of deliberate stage management. I guess I'm a sucker for that hero stuff."

"You and millions of excited Bagestanis, Marta. And who knows? Maybe it's really true."

"Let's hope so. Well, Barry, and then just three days ago we had the wonderful spectacle of the wedding of Sultan al Jawadi to his fiancée, the actress Dana Morningstar, who saved his life during that assassination attempt in London. And that's a day to remember, too."

The library film showed Dana and Ashraf standing under a magnificent arched doorway covered in painted green tile. "And there's another source of happiness for the majority of Bagestanis," a reporter was saying softly. "The wedding of their new sultan and sultana is the first ceremony to take place in the newly restored Central Mosque. For almost thirty years, it has been a museum, and an army of craftspeople and artisans has been working day and night for weeks to restore it to its original use. And here they come."

The film showed Ashraf and Dana stepping out into the bright sunlight and waving at the cheering crowds. Dana was wearing a beautiful, flowing, pure white *shal-*

war kamees, with white flowers in her long dark hair. Ashraf wore a turquoise silk high-necked jacket.

"The bride deliberately chose not to wear any kind of veil, as a signal that there will be no dress laws in the new Bagestan. It's a symbol of the equal freedom and rights that women will share with men in Bagestan under the new government. Sultan Ashraf is known to have asked religious leaders throughout the country to work together on a new interpretation of Qu'ranic law for the modern world...."

The film gave way to the studio talking heads again.

"And now, Marta, after three days of wedding celebrations, the Bagestanis are taking to the streets again to celebrate the formal coronation of their sultan and sultana. This is the first joint rule of a husband and wife in the history of Bagestan," said Barry.

"Yes, it's a resoundingly historic moment to add to all the other historic moments in Bagestan. I am sure this year will be a landmark year in the Bagestani calendar for decades to come. And Andrea is at the ceremony which is just about to take place in the Throne Room of the Old Palace...Andrea, are you there?"

"Yes, Marta, we're just outside the Throne Room waiting for the ceremony to begin. Through the doors behind me is the room where for centuries the Sultans of Bagestan held court for ordinary citizens, and that is where the ceremony will take place. Inside, for the first time in history, are two thrones. The new monarchs will be crowned by the Nazim al Zaman, the former Grand Wazir of Sultan Ashraf's grandfather, who is now eighty-eight years old.

"We've still got quite a long wait, so let me remind the viewers that after the ceremony Bagestan is going to be indulging in one massive, country-wide party that will last another three days. And when it's over Bagestanis will have been celebrating for a week in all. A very traditional period of celebration in Bagestan.

"Through the doors in the other direction are several interconnecting rooms, through all of which the royal procession will pass on the way to the Throne Room. And each of those rooms is filling up with the wedding guests, who are now arriving in large numbers. There will be representatives of governments and monarchies from around the world who have come to witness this historic occasion, including all the princes of the Barakat Emirates and their wives.

"Every city and town in the country has sent one representative, chosen by lot. Also invited to share the celebration, we are told, are all those who assisted the al Jawadi family in their campaign to regain the throne. Among the guests on his own merits is the new sultana's father. General Loghatullah is a hero in his own right. He is credited with single-handedly saving the royal family from extinction back in 1969."

"It must run in the blood, Andrea."

"Yes, the new sultana is going to find herself very popular with her people, from all that I've heard in the streets. That photograph of her on the floor of the restaurant, protecting a wounded Ashraf al Jawadi, has been blazoned all over the front pages here...."

It was another half hour before the trumpets announced to those who waited that the pageant was about to begin, and silence fell. There was a long pause, with absolute quiet. Then a voice called out something indecipherable, and there was a loud rapping, and two pages stepped from their posts to open two massive, arched double doors.

Two more opened the next doors, and two more the next, until there was a passage, carpeted in red, leading through a dozen rooms of the palace from an antechamber all the way to the Throne Room. Each of the rooms was lined with rows of seats and crowded with spectators.

The trumpets sounded again. Then an old man in white robes stepped through the door of the antechamber and set out along the passage. He carried a richly jewelled and decorated Qu'ran open on his two outspread hands. Behind him came a dozen men and a dozen women in fabulous costumes of bright silks and jewels. They walked in two rows, and first in line were Najib al Makhtoum and Haroun al Jawadi, carrying two circlets of gold on purple velvet cushions.

The magnificent procession moved slowly along the red carpet that ran from room to room, towards the Throne Room and the raised dais within.

Behind them, side by side, walking slowly under the weight of their cloaks, came Sultana Dana Morningstar Loghatullah and Sultan Ashraf Durran ibn Wafiq ibn Hafzuddin al Jawadi.

The sultana wore a lustrous heavy cloth-of-gold cloak, luxuriously ruched and latticed with thousands of pearls and caught over her shoulders with a double rope of gleaming pearls. Her hair was woven into a heavy chignon threaded with pearls and diamonds, and massive pearl drops hung from her ears. Her simply cut shimmering dress was also cloth of gold, as were the slippers that peeped out from under its hem. Behind her stretched a train several yards long.

Beside her, the dark-haired handsome sultan also wore a suit of cloth of gold, with high-necked jacket. Strings of luscious pearls were looped across his chest from shoulder to waist, held in place by a giant emerald on his breast. His cloth-of-gold cloak was purfled with pearls and diamonds, and his train matched the length of hers.

And on his hand, the diamond ring called the al Jawadi Rose glittered and glowed with a magic few could believe.

Four pages dressed in white and gold walked on either side of the long trains.

As they passed from room to room among the silently standing guests, the sun falling through the tall windows caught the gold so that the royal couple glowed in the centre of a shimmering halo, giving a touch of unreality to the scene.

For those watching, it was a once-in-a-lifetime experience. For many, it was their first taste of such splendour, and they would be forever changed by the moment.

In one room, a woman reached for the hand of an elegant, white-haired old man, and clutched it for as long as the golden vision lasted. When the royal procession had moved through the doors into the next chamber, she continued in silence for a long, breathless moment, staring up at the monitor which showed its further progress. Then she sighed, turned her head a little and whispered in French, "Oh, Monsieur Saint-Julien! Who would have imagined it? Can you believe that this is not a dream? Did you see the ring? Is it not magnificent? And to think that we contributed, even so little, to this wonderful occasion."

The old man whispered back, "Marthe, we are in danger of becoming the worst bores in the region. We will tell the story until we have one foot in the grave, and even on our deathbeds we will say, *You know, I was once of material assistance to the Sultan of Bagestan's*

*brother, when he was on a most important mission to
find the ring they called the al Jawadi Rose. Did I ever
tell you about the coronation…?''*

When the procession reached the Throne Room, the
aged Grand Wazir climbed three shallow steps to the
first level of the dais and turned to face the long passage.
One step above was the platform where the thrones sat.

Twelve women and ten men filed along the sides of
the dais on the first two steps, but Haroun al Jawadi and
Najib al Makhtoum, carrying the crowns, climbed up
and stood one on each side of the Grand Wazir.

Then, with the trumpets sounding triumphantly, the
royal couple stepped through the entrance to the Throne
Room and moved along the carpet towards the dais, and
then up the first three steps. There they knelt.

''Bismullah arrahman arrahim,'' intoned the old wazir.

In the streets, too, there was silence, as people stood
watching the ceremony on the large public television
screens that were relics of the old, hated regime. Cars
slowed and pulled over, their drivers stopping to listen
as the magic of the day translated even over the radio
waves.

In the Throne Room, after more than thirty years, the
crown was at last placed on the head of an al Jawadi
again, and, for the first time in history, on his wife's
head. Then the newly crowned sultan and sultana rose,
and moving up the last step together, turned and sat on
the thrones. The band played the old national anthem,
and all the assembled sang so loudly the domed roof
seemed to lift.

When the anthem was finished, the palace erupted
with cheering.

Then there was the procession of various officials,

who marched to the throne to bend their knee in a sign of allegiance.

And then, as the sultan and sultana still sat side by side, smiling at the assembled and at each other, and the guests sank to their seats, an old woman, who was among the representatives of all the cities and towns of the country, remained standing, and walked forward to the throne. She held up one hand, and one of the sultan's newly appointed Cup Companions leapt forward, but the sultan's hand on his shoulder arrested him.

"Ya Sultan!" cried the old woman in a country patois. "I come to you from the troubled citizens of Skandar!" And then everyone saw that what she held up was a roll of paper. "I bring a petition to the sultan! Please help us in our troubles!" And she bent and placed the little scroll on a step of the dais.

She had not returned to her seat before a man followed her. He, too, held up a paper and begged for it to be read. And then all eyes were turned to the red carpet, for along it were coming others, and still others, until a steady stream of those who had suffered under Ghasib's yoke came forward to offer petitions in the Throne Room, exactly as their forebears had done in times past.

The room was silent with astonished awe.

Many of the petitioners laid their petitions specifically before the Sultana, begging her intercession. And at the end of an hour, there was a mound of papers, some torn and dirty and almost illiterate, some neat and scrupulously written, some in envelopes, some rolled, some flat, some tied with bits of ribbon, before each of the thrones.

The sultan and the sultana sat and waited until everyone who wished to leave a petition had been able to do so. Then, at a signal, the newly appointed Cup Companions of each of them stepped forward and gathered up every petition.

Only then did the sultan and sultana, their golden crowns around their temples, rise from their seats and step down from the dais and walk back along the red carpet, leading the guests to the great banqueting hall where a feast awaited them.

Late that night, when the feasting and celebration were over for the day, Ashraf and Dana were alone again. Dana, her hair spread out around her shoulders, and wearing a tiny slip of silk, lay across the wide bed on her stomach, a neat leather box beside her, reading from a paper.

Ash stood at a window, looking out over the courtyard where his father had played as a child, and his father before him, for so many generations. The great tree that his father had told him about when he was a child, against all expectations, was still there.

It's done, Grandfather, he whispered to the old man. *Now I must hope to be granted the wisdom to do it well.*

"I don't believe it!" Dana muttered, frowning at the paper she was reading. "What does this word mean— *manba?*"

"It means a well."

"I thought so! It's appalling! One of Ghasib's functionaries was insulted by some member of this community, and in revenge he slaughtered some animals and threw the carcasses in their *well.* To deliberately poison it! And they haven't been able to clear it, and for two years they've had to walk miles to the next village to get the water there, and…Ash, what would it take? A crane?"

"We'll have to send an engineer to assess the situation."

Shaking her head, Dana set the petition back in the box, and got to her feet. She approached the window and stood beside him. A full moon was riding high in a cloudless sky. Below, the courtyard was in darkness.

"What are you looking at?" she murmured, as his mood stole over her.

"Do you see that tree out there?"

"That big one?"

He nodded. "My father used to get up inside that tree to hide from his tutors. And none of them ever discovered his hiding place."

She caught her lip between her teeth and smiled. "And it's still there!"

"It's still there."

"You never got a chance to do that," she said softly.

"No."

"Maybe your sons will."

He turned to face her, his hands lifting to her shoulders. She looked fearlessly into his eyes, ready for their shared future. And he knew that she was the wife every man dreams of—a partner for the good times and the bad. Who would face both troubles and successes with the same confident strength.

"Yes," he said, "*insha'Allah,* our sons will. And our daughters, too."

And he drew his wife into his arms and set his mouth on hers.

*   *   *   *   *

THE FORTUNES OF TEXAS

invite you to meet

THE LOST HEIRS

Silhouette Desire's scintillating new miniseries, featuring the beloved

FORTUNES OF TEXAS

and six of your favorite authors.

A Most Desirable M.D.—June 2001
by Anne Marie Winston (SD #1371)

The Pregnant Heiress—July 2001
by Eileen Wilks (SD #1378)

Baby of Fortune—August 2001
by Shirley Rogers (SD #1384)

Fortune's Secret Daughter—September 2001
by Barbara McCauley (SD #1390)

Her Boss's Baby—October 2001
by Cathleen Galitz (SD #1396)

Did You Say Twins?!—December 2001
by Maureen Child (SD #1408)

And be sure to watch for *Gifts of Fortune*,
Silhouette's exciting new single title,
on sale November 2001

*Don't miss these unforgettable romances…
available at your favorite retail outlet.*

Where love comes alive™

Visit Silhouette at www.eHarlequin.com   SDFOT

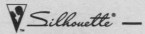

SILHOUETTE®
MAKES YOU
A STAR!

Feel like a star with Silhouette.

We will fly you and a guest to New York City for an exciting weekend stay at a glamorous 5-star hotel. Experience a refreshing day at one of New York's trendiest spas and have your photo taken by a professional. Plus, receive $1,000 U.S. spending money!

Flowers...long walks...dinner for two... how does Silhouette Books make romance come alive for you?

Send us a script, with 500 words or less, along with visuals (only drawings, magazine cutouts or photographs or combination thereof). Show us how Silhouette Makes Your Love Come Alive. Be creative and have fun. No purchase necessary. All entries must be clearly marked with your name, address and telephone number. All entries will become property of Silhouette and are not returnable. **Contest closes September 28, 2001.**

Please send your entry to: **Silhouette Makes You a Star!**

In U.S.A.
P.O. Box 9069
Buffalo, NY, 14269-9069

In Canada
P.O. Box 637
Fort Erie, ON, L2A 5X3

Look for contest details on the next page, by visiting www.eHarlequin.com or request a copy by sending a self-addressed envelope to the applicable address above. Contest open to Canadian and U.S. residents who are 18 or over. Void where prohibited.

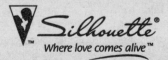

Silhouette®
Where love comes alive™

Our lucky winner's photo will appear in a Silhouette ad. Join the fun!

HARLEQUIN "SILHOUETTE MAKES YOU A STAR!" CONTEST 1308
OFFICIAL RULES
NO PURCHASE NECESSARY TO ENTER

1. To enter, follow directions published in the offer to which you are responding. Contest begins June 1, 2001, and ends on September 28, 2001. Entries must be postmarked by September 28, 2001, and received by October 5, 2001. Enter by hand-printing (or typing) on an 8 ½" x 11" piece of paper your name, address (including zip code), contest number/name and attaching a script containing 500 words or less, along with drawings, photographs or magazine cutouts, or combinations thereof (i.e., collage) on no larger than 9" x 12" piece of paper, describing how the Silhouette books make romance come alive for you. Mail via first-class mail to: Harlequin "Silhouette Makes You a Star!" Contest 1308, (in the U.S.) P.O. Box 9069, Buffalo, NY 14269-9069, (in Canada) P.O. Box 637, Fort Erie, Ontario, Canada L2A 5X3. Limit one entry per person, household or organization.

2. Contests will be judged by a panel of members of the Harlequin editorial, marketing and public relations staff. Fifty percent of criteria will be judged against script and fifty percent will be judged against drawing, photographs and/or magazine cutouts. Judging criteria will be based on the following:

   - Sincerity—25%
   - Originality and Creativity—50%
   - Emotionally Compelling—25%

   In the event of a tie, duplicate prizes will be awarded. Decisions of the judges are final.

3. All entries become the property of Torstar Corp. and may be used for future promotional purposes. Entries will not be returned. No responsibility is assumed for lost, late, illegible, incomplete, inaccurate, nondelivered or misdirected mail.

4. Contest open only to residents of the U.S. (except Puerto Rico) and Canada who are 18 years of age or older, and is void wherever prohibited by law; all applicable laws and regulations apply. Any litigation within the Province of Quebec respecting the conduct or organization of a publicity contest may be submitted to the Régie des alcools, des courses et des jeux for a ruling. Any litigation respecting the awarding of a prize may be submitted to the Régie des alcools, des courses et des jeux only for the purpose of helping the parties reach a settlement. Employees and immediate family members of Torstar Corp. and D. L. Blair, Inc., their affiliates, subsidiaries and all other agencies, entities and persons connected with the use, marketing or conduct of this contest are not eligible to enter. Taxes on prizes are the sole responsibility of the winner. Acceptance of any prize offered constitutes permission to use winner's name, photograph or other likeness for the purposes of advertising, trade and promotion on behalf of Torstar Corp., its affiliates and subsidiaries without further compensation to the winner, unless prohibited by law.

5. Winner will be determined no later than November 30, 2001, and will be notified by mail. Winner will be required to sign and return an Affidavit of Eligibility/Release of Liability/Publicity Release form within 15 days after winner notification. Noncompliance within that time period may result in disqualification and an alternative winner may be selected. All travelers must execute a Release of Liability prior to ticketing and must possess required travel documents (e.g., passport, photo ID) where applicable. Trip must be booked by December 31, 2001, and completed within one year of notification. No substitution of prize permitted by winner. Torstar Corp. and D. L. Blair, Inc., their parents, affiliates and subsidiaries are not responsible for errors in printing of contest, entries and/or game pieces. In the event of printing or other errors that may result in unintended prize values or duplication of prizes, all affected game pieces or entries shall be null and void. **Purchase or acceptance of a product offer does not improve your chances of winning.**

6. Prizes: (1) Grand Prize—A 2-night/3-day trip for two (2) to New York City, including round-trip coach air transportation nearest winner's home and hotel accommodations (double occupancy) at The Plaza Hotel, a glamorous afternoon makeover at a trendy New York spa, $1,000 in U.S. spending money and an opportunity to have a professional photo taken and appear in a Silhouette advertisement (approximate retail value: $7,000). (10) Ten Runner-Up Prizes of gift packages (retail value $50 ea.). Prizes consist of only those items listed as part of the prize. Limit one prize per person. Prize is valued in U.S. currency.

7. For the name of the winner (available after December 31, 2001) send a self-addressed, stamped envelope to: Harlequin "Silhouette Makes You a Star!" Contest 1197 Winners, P.O. Box 4200 Blair, NE 68009-4200 or you may access the www.eHarlequin.com Web site through February 28, 2002.

Contest sponsored by Torstar Corp., P.O. Box 9042, Buffalo, NY 14269-9042.

SRMYAS2

If you enjoyed what you just read,
then we've got an offer you can't resist!

Take 2 bestselling
love stories FREE!
Plus get a FREE surprise gift!

Clip this page and mail it to Silhouette Reader Service™

IN U.S.A.
3010 Walden Ave.
P.O. Box 1867
Buffalo, N.Y. 14240-1867

IN CANADA
P.O. Box 609
Fort Erie, Ontario
L2A 5X3

YES! Please send me 2 free Silhouette Desire® novels and my free surprise gift. After receiving them, if I don't wish to receive anymore, I can return the shipping statement marked cancel. If I don't cancel, I will receive 6 brand-new novels every month, before they're available in stores! In the U.S.A., bill me at the bargain price of $3.34 plus 25¢ shipping and handling per book and applicable sales tax, if any*. In Canada, bill me at the bargain price of $3.74 plus 25¢ shipping and handling per book and applicable taxes**. That's the complete price and a savings of at least 10% off the cover prices—what a great deal! I understand that accepting the 2 free books and gift places me under no obligation ever to buy any books. I can always return a shipment and cancel at any time. Even if I never buy another book from Silhouette, the 2 free books and gift are mine to keep forever.

225 SEN DFNS
326 SEN DFNT

Name	(PLEASE PRINT)	
Address	Apt.#	
City	State/Prov.	Zip/Postal Code

* Terms and prices subject to change without notice. Sales tax applicable in N.Y.
** Canadian residents will be charged applicable provincial taxes and GST.
All orders subject to approval. Offer limited to one per household and not valid to current Silhouette Desire® subscribers.
® are registered trademarks of Harlequin Enterprises Limited.

DES01   ©1998 Harlequin Enterprises Limited

COMING SOON...

AN EXCITING
OPPORTUNITY TO SAVE
ON THE PURCHASE OF
HARLEQUIN AND
SILHOUETTE BOOKS!

*DETAILS TO FOLLOW
IN OCTOBER 2001!*

YOU WON'T WANT TO MISS IT!

PHQ401